Hall, Lynn
    Too near the sun

Too Near the SUN

stefan Martin

Too Near the SUN

Lynn Hall

WOODCUTS BY STEFAN MARTIN

FOLLETT PUBLISHING COMPANY
CHICAGO   NEW YORK

G72-W1672

OTHER BOOKS BY THE AUTHOR

THE SHY ONES
THE SECRET OF STONEHOUSE
RIDE A WILD DREAM

ISBN O 695-40069-X Titan binding
ISBN O 695-80069-8 Trade binding

Library of Congress Catalog Card Number: 76-85939

First Printing

D

FOR SANDY

Too Near the SUN

THE DREAM

A few miles east of Corning, in southwestern Iowa, there is a relic of a country graveyard. The few passersby who notice it assume that it's an ordinary graveyard.

Not many notice it, though. From U.S. Highway 34 all that can be seen are four trees rising from the center of a high, flat pasture. Two of the three wild cherry trees were split and deformed in a tornado sixty years ago. The other tree, the old box elder, is a standing skeleton. None of its four trunks has shown life for several years.

Under this square of trees only three headstones and parts of a fourth can still be found. The other stones, more than fifty of them, have been rooted under by hogs, or hauled away to clear the pasture for the seasons when it's planted in oats. Some say a few of the headstones have been put to use in a sidewalk for a neighboring farmhouse.

The three remaining stones lie almost hidden by the long grass. Under a crust of mud and manure are the inscriptions written in French. The largest stone bears the names "Louise and Hippolyte Claudy" and the inscription "En souvenir de nos mère et père, décédés à Icarie."

It was more than a handful of French settlers that "died in Icaria." A dream died there too, and it was no small dream.

It began in France in 1840, when a lawyer and politician, Étienne Cabet, published a book called *Voyage to Icaria*. The book described Cabet's vision of a perfect society, a world in which every man worked for the common good and everyone was given all he needed by the commune. No individual in Cabet's Icaria would own anything, so there would be no jealousy, no theft, no greed. Marriages would be arranged by the commune, eliminating all the problems and unhappiness caused by romantic love. Every adult would be assigned the duties he was best suited to perform in the common interest. All food, clothing, and other necessities would be doled out by the commune, which would own everything, so that neither poverty nor selfish wealth could exist. And of course there would be no religious nonsense, because Icaria would recognize no power greater than the commune.

From each according to his ability; to each according to his need. This was the dream, the paradise on earth. Perfect peace and harmony. Perfect communism.

Because life in France at that time was far from any sort of paradise, Cabet's dream took root in the hungry imaginations of the French, and grew. In 1847 he and sixty-nine others pooled their money and bought from a European land agent a large tract of land in Texas. The Icarians, as they called themselves now, settled first in Texas and then in Nauvoo, Illinois, in the snug stone houses recently abandoned by the Mormons who had moved on to Utah. Later, after Cabet's death in 1856, about thirty of the remaining families moved west to the lush and lonely prairie of western Iowa.

Here they would be safe, they thought, from the creeping evil of the rest of the world. Here, on their three thousand acres of the most fertile earth in the world, they could live out their lives with a minimum of work and no worry, no unpleasantness of any kind. There would be lovely, sturdy homes with ample heat and running water, busy factories, productive farms, fine schools, theaters and amusement palaces, elegant pleasure grounds and the leisure-time to enjoy them. There would be culture. Beauty. Feasts and dancing and perfect harmony.

The graveyard with its dead box elder tree; two farmhouses built from parts of Icarian buildings; and some oddly shaped bricks that occasionally turn up in the spring plowing of the field nearest the old mill site—these are all that remain of Étienne Cabet's dream. For, like the mythical Icarus who soared too near the sun and melted his wings of wax, Cabet tried to fly too high. He, in his attempt to create perfection on earth, overlooked the imperfection of human nature.

This is the story of the summer when the wings of Cabet's dream began to melt.

CHAPTER ONE

The sun was warm on Armel's shoulders and the
back of his neck, and it glared on the pages of his
book. He sat in the center of a six-foot gap in the
hedge that separated the sheep pasture from the
cornfield behind him. He had been posted here for
several weeks, and on days when he didn't have
a book, he enjoyed the view.

From the high plateau of the cornfield the ground

fell away in a sharp grassy slope following the curve of the Nodaway River that ran a half-mile to the north. The slope, too steep for anything but grazing sheep, was dotted with the soft green of trees just beginning to leaf out and the gray masses of Armel's one hundred and twenty-seven ewes. The ewes weren't really his, of course. They belonged to the commune.

At the bottom of the slope the ground leveled abruptly and lay in a flat, fertile band of bottomland. A dark line of trees and the roofs of the sawmill and the gristmill were all that could be seen of the river from this distance. To Armel's left, at the top of the ridge and some distance away, were the barns; beyond them stood the cluster of buildings that made up the commune of Icaria.

It was April, 1875, nearly twenty years after the idealistic Icarians, following Étienne Cabet's dream of a perfect society, had founded their communal settlement in this quiet Iowa valley.

Now the wind rose slightly, lifting Armel's dark hair and rippling the shirt across his back. He was sitting on the rim of the ridge, with his feet comfortably downhill. His boots were off, not because it was really that warm yet, but because Citizen Fremont had made them too narrow through the toes again and Armel's toenails had begun to dig little gashes in their neighboring toes. Besides, the grass felt good. It was short and fine and full of tiny pastel wild flowers. Idly he stripped the heads off the flowers with his toes while he read.

The book lay heavy against his denim legs. He shifted it up an inch or so and turned the page. The shadow of a cloud moved across the pasture and Armel and the book, but he didn't notice. Nor did he hear the subtle difference in the rustling of the trees down the hill. He was totally absorbed in the case history he was reading. The book was one of several hundred that had made up Papa's law library back in France, before Armel's time. On the flyleaf the words "Property of Franz Dupree" had been crossed out. Below them, in the strident hand of Étienne Cabet himself, was written "Property of Icaria."

As one of the ewes wandered toward Armel and the break in the hedge, he tossed a clod of earth in front of her and said, "Get back, silly," all without losing his place on the page.

When he came to the end of the case history, he stood, marking his place in the book with one finger. He held the volume against his ribs with his left arm and drew his face into a frown. His right arm shot out to point directly into the face of the nearest sheep.

"Are you aware, sir, of the penalty for perjury in this court? And you still maintain that you have no knowledge of the defendant's whereabouts at the time this hideous crime was committed?" His voice rose in beautiful scorn.

The ewe stared at him. Slowly her jaws stopped moving.

Armel turned toward the cluster of sheep grazing a few yards away. Now his voice held just a touch of acid humor. "Gentlemen of the jury, this witness is evidently having a little fun with us this afternoon. I'm sure he wouldn't deliberately insult your intelligence by asking you to believe such a story."

The witness had gone back to her grazing and was moving slowly down the slope.

"Your Honor, I demand you hold this witness in contempt of court!" Armel's demand was answered by a sudden rumbling crescendo of thunder. He laughed at the thunder's perfect timing; then, waving his clenched fist over his head, he looked up at the darkening sky and shouted, "Your Honor, I object!"

From behind him a voice said, "You'd do better to quit objecting and get these ewes penned up, son. This old hedge won't keep them in if they decide to get storm-panicked." It was Citizen Bronner.

"Yes, sir." Armel didn't bother to be embarrassed. Citizen Bronner had heard him talking to the sheep often enough before. He sat down to force his feet back into his boots. "How about the pigs? Shall we get them in, too?"

If Bronner heard the question, he ignored it. He walked along the hedge toward the barns, a stout, white-haired figure whose farm clothes hung on his erect body as though they were not his, even after all these years. As he walked away, an occasional word escaped his silent stream of conversation and came out aloud, unnoticed.

Armel watched the retreating Bronner and thought, No use calling after him about the pigs. He's in ancient Rome by now or giving a lecture someplace. Oh well, the pigs'll be all right out in the timber, but I'd better get these ewes in out of the rain. And the chickens.

The poultry house stood among the trees between the sheep shed and the larger barns to the south. When Armel got there, Bronner was, in his ponderous way, chasing elusive white hens that squawked and flapped through the grass.

A little distance away Emil James and his son Alexis stood watching Bronner. Alexis was eighteen, just a year older than Armel, and the only boy in Icaria who was near Armel's age. That fact didn't forge any bonds between them.

Armel glanced from the two Jameses to Citizen Bronner, stooping awkwardly toward a hen. "Why don't you help him?" he snapped.

The two men, father and son, looked vaguely at each other. Alexis shrugged. "Chickens ain't *our* responsibility, Armel. We're field men, remember?"

Armel flared. "These chickens are just as much yours as they are mine, and when they get rained on and get sick and die, *you're* going to get hungry for eggs just like the rest of us." But he knew there was no point in arguing with those two. The rain was falling steadily now, and the hens were still to be caught.

While Armel and Bronner trotted, dodged, and dove after the hens, their audience grew to four. Citizen Peron and Citizen Ponte came to stand in the shelter of the oaks with the Jameses and to watch the hen-chasers.

By the time the last screeching bird was caught and tossed into the poultry house, Armel was soaked through. Gooseflesh rose on his arms in response to the chilled breeze. He stood with Citizen Bronner just inside the door of the horse barn, waiting for the first fury of the rain to wear itself out.

"I'd like to knock their heads together," he muttered, looking out toward the four figures under the trees. Bronner was silent, staring out through the slanted silver curtain of rain.

Armel relaxed against the door frame. From

the dark cave of the barn behind him came the warm smells of horses and hay. The wind was letting up now; the rain was a sibilant whisper in the leaves of the trees. Without turning his head, Armel saw the profile of the man beside him. Bronner's head was shiny-bald on top, with a white fringe around the back that looped over his ears and became his beard, one of the longest, fullest, whitest beards in Icaria. His sister had said once that Bronner's beard looked like a napkin looped over his ears and tied behind his head. Nearly buried in the profuse beard was an oversized, low-swooping, ornately carved briar pipe with its bowl turned around now to keep the rain out. It had always been a wonder to Armel that Bronner's beard hadn't long ago been burned away.

Bronner glanced up at him. "What are you grinning about, pup?"

"I was just noticing that I'm taller than you now."

"You have been ever since they assigned you to me."

"Nearly two years now."

"Two years." Bronner reached for the long matches in his shirt pocket and twisted the pipe's bowl around to smoking position.

"No smoking in the barn," Armel reminded him. Bronner sighed and put the matches away.

The whish of the rain began to mesmerize Armel. He yawned and recrossed his arms. From the stalls behind them came the thud of hoof against wall. Armel said, "How many horses are they taking to Shenandoah?"

Bronner's eyes were focused somewhere beyond the poplars that lined the gardens behind the commune. He was silent for a long time, and when he spoke, it was something that sounded like "window man."

"Citizen Bronner? I said, how many horses are they going to take to Shenandoah to sell. Do you know?"

"Uh? Oh. Why, three, I believe, or else five. No, three."

Armel looked back through the dimness of the barn to the row of high, rounded rumps of the horses in their stalls. They were all handsomely dappled grays, all fine Percherons descended from the French stock brought over by the original Icarians.

"I wonder how much we get for them," Armel mused aloud.

Bronner's voice lost its usual foggy quality. He snapped, "If I were you, pup, I'd just appreciate the fact that you'll never have to worry about money, or how much you're going to get for something, or where your next meal comes from. You young ones don't know how things were before. You don't appreciate what we have here."

"You're right," Armel said. He didn't want to irritate Bronner, especially now, when he was working up to asking Bronner for a favor.

"The reason I was asking how many horses they're taking to Shenandoah—I just—well, I'm seventeen this year." Bronner was gazing out past the poplars again. "I talked it over with Papa, and at Meeting tonight he's going to ask if they'll take me with them to Shenandoah, because Alexis and Cabet got to go when they were seventeen. And if they're taking three horses, they could probably use some more help."

He waited, but Bronner had nothing to say.

"Bronner?"

"I'm listening."

"Well? Will you tell them you can get along without me for a week?"

Bronner's lips moved as he made soft sucking sounds in his pipe. "Oh, yes, I suppose you must go, if the others did. I'll tell them I can get along without you, if you'll make me a promise." He turned toward Armel, and his eyes were intense upon Armel's face. "Promise me you'll keep your head on straight?"

The concern in Bronner's face had a quality of loving in it that warmed and embarrassed Armel. "How do you mean, keep my head on straight?"

Bronner turned away. "You know. Valmor."

"Oh well, *Valmor*. That was something else again. I promise to keep my head on straight. That make you happy?" His voice was light again.

Bronner just smiled.

"Oh, one other thing," Armel said. "Don't forget tonight, when they make out the list of nursery stock to get, be sure and order the replacement plants for where the hedge is dying. I don't especially care to spend the whole summer standing in that hole in the hedge."

"Hedge replacement plants. Yes. I'll remember to bring that up. Thank you, Mel. I don't know what I'd do without you." He said it seriously, acknowledging what both of them knew, that the small stock would lead precarious lives if they had to depend only on the Small Stock Chairman.

"Let's go," Armel said suddenly. "The rain is letting up."

He jogged across the grass to the sheep shed for his book, then caught up with Bronner as he was crossing the road. The man touched Armel's sleeve and motioned toward the sky. Against a background of blue-gray clouds, still raining to the west, a rainbow arched. It was one of the most brilliant Armel had ever seen.

Directly below the pastel arch lay the buildings of the commune. The dining hall stood in the center, a solid white frame rectangle, two stories high and nearly as long as the horse barn. Around it, in a rough parallelogram, were the houses and shops. Seven frame houses now, not counting the bakery and the washhouse. All were small white rectangles, less than six months old. The sawdust and wood chips had not completely disappeared with the melting of the winter snow. Scattered among and behind the frame houses were fifteen log cabins. Four of the better cabins were still occupied; the others were gradually being torn down or converted to storerooms.

At the door of the dining hall Armel left Bronner and went inside. The building's one room on the main floor was filled with the smells of supper. He stopped for a moment to sort them. Ham. Hot German potato salad—must be Citizenne Hawbaker's week to help cook. Some kind of greens—dandelion? And of course the strong hot smell of café au lait. His stomach squeezed up a message of empty pain.

I'll just take this book back, he thought; then run home and get out of these wet clothes and be back in time for supper. He loped up the spiral stairs of the dining hall three at a time.

The east half of the second floor was a storage area; the west half was divided into a large sewing and tailoring shop and a smaller, darker room that served as the library. A few years ago Armel had built shelves along one wall of the cubicle, and had arranged his favorite books on them. The rest were piled in leaning stacks on the floor. He stepped over and around the stacks, which he knew by heart, and slid his book into the black space that waited for it.

I'm going to get these darned boots off, too, right now, he decided.

The leather was stiffening as it dried, making the boots nearly unbearable. He wrenched them off. On the stairs he paused to wish briefly that the stairway, with its inviting spiraled railing, had been built years ago, while he was small enough to get away with sliding down it. He stopped a few steps from the bottom, paused, threw a leg over the rail.

"Armel Dupree, you act your age, now, and get down off that railing before you break it." Citizenne Hawbaker frowned out at him from the pantry in the end of the room, where she was handing stacks of tin plates to her two children.

He sighed and dismounted. "Just like having a dozen mothers around here." He said it just loudly enough for the two little Hawbakers to hear. Rolfe and Gretchen looked up from their stacks of plates and allowed themselves a quick giggle before they went back to the serious business of setting the tables.

For a moment he watched the children as they moved among the round black-walnut tables. They aren't children so much as miniature adults, he thought. He remembered how it used to be when he and Jeannie and Cabet were small enough to have table-setting duty. It had been a game with them, a race to see who could get his four tables laid out first, with no corrections from Maman when she came around to check on the neatness of each setting. Knife blades had to be turned out, café cups set with their handles to the right.

He remembered the way Maman used to look at the three of them sometimes—four of them when Valmor was there, too. She'd smile at each, at all, and it seemed to Armel that her children were giving Maman some sort of precious gift when they laughed together. It was the only gift they'd ever been able to give her, and after Valmor left, the gift had never been complete, no matter how hard he and Jeannie and Cabet tried. He wondered if Citizenne Hawbaker's children ever gave her the gift of their affection for each other—or whether she needed it the way Maman seemed to.

Rolfe and Gretchen marched back to the pantry, single file. Armel started for the door, but turned toward the pantry when he heard Maman's voice. She was calling down the dumbwaiter to the women in the basement-kitchen. When she turned around, her square face was red from bending over.

"Ah, Armel, good. We were just needing someone to take Catherine's tray over to her. She's having a little trouble with her back. Then see if you can find Jeannie, and tell her to stop at the bakery and bring the bread when she comes."

"I don't think I'll have time, Maman. I've got to change my boots and get cleaned up and . . ."

His words were lost in the creak of the dumbwaiter as it brought up a large tin tray and delivered it into Maman's hands. The food on the tray was covered by a damask tablecloth, creamy with age and folded several times.

"Here you go, Armel. Tell Catherine we're all sorry about her back. And don't forget to tell Jeannie about the bread."

With resignation he took the tray and pushed out of the dining hall into the evening sunshine.

Catherine Noir's cabin was at the far end of the commune, near the orchards. It was one of the largest and best of the remaining log cabins. It was, in fact, the place where Armel had been born. Papa had built it seventeen years ago, when the settlement first came to the Nodaway Valley; the roof had been on for just three days before Armel's birth. Last fall, when the Duprees' frame house was completed, Catherine was moved into their old cabin so that hers could fall apart completely, as it had been doing gradually for years.

Catherine Noir was the onus of Icaria, the one member who did absolutely nothing to help anyone. She had been a servant in France for a family who joined the original Icarian pilgrims. The couple she served had died twenty years ago, when Icaria was in Texas. Catherine, then in her sixties and utterly helpless to make a life on her own, had stayed with the Icarians and allowed the members to build a cabin for her, carry her meals from the dining hall, and pity her for her various illnesses.

At the cabin door Armel knocked, then pushed on through the doorway. The wood-and-mud smell of the cabin survived from his childhood, in spite of Catherine and her uncleanliness. The whitewashed walls of the tiny room still showed the crayoned birds and horses and cows that he and Jeannie had put there so painstakingly, years ago. His birds were all red-winged blackbirds. Jeannie's were all bluebirds.

"Ah, young Dupree, is it?" Catherine's voice quavered up weakly from the bed in the corner. "I won't be able to eat any of it. My back is broken, you know. Did they remember to cut up the meat for me?" As Armel set the tray on the packing-crate table beside the bed, Catherine's blue-veined hand came slowly out of hiding to lift the edge of the cloth. Satisfied that the meat was cut up, she sank back and closed her eyes. The strip of sun that lay across the bed showed her scalp, pink and shining, through her sparse hair.

"I'm sorry about your back, Catherine." He found it difficult to put the proper sincerity into the words.

"You're a dear boy, Cabet. Your maman is my only friend, you know."

"I'm Armel."

She opened her eyes to glare at him. Then, smiling feebly, she motioned to the row of pegs in the wall at the foot of the bed.

"Bring the shawl, Cabet. I want you to give it to your maman. She's my only friend."

Trying to hide his impatience, trying not to limp as his toenails gouged away inside his stiff boots, he brought the familiar old shawl. Its maroon paisley weave was a part of his childhood, just as the crayoned birds on the wall were.

"That's a fine boy. Take the shawl, now, and give it to your maman."

As he escaped from the cabin and closed the door, he heard the sudden creak of the rope bed-springs, the scrape of the table, the clatter of tin dishes on the tray. He wrapped the shawl around his shoulders, Indian-fashion, and loped across the grass toward home.

Jeannie was just coming out of the Dupree house. Under one arm she carried a bundle of pale, dampened straws, the same bundle that had been with her all week. Her sleek head was bent; her hands worked the braid of straw that emerged from

28

the bundle. Her eyes were on the braid, so she didn't see her brother until he called.

She glanced up, noticed the shawl, and smiled at him. "Did Catherine give her shawl to Maman again?"

He nodded solemnly and began to fold the shawl. "Maman is her one and only friend in the whole world again. This week. Oh, listen, Maman said for you to stop and get the bread on your way to supper. It's still at the bakery."

A shadow of dismay crossed her face. She glanced from her straw bundle to Armel. "Can't you get it, Mel? I've got to get this one more hat done before they go to Shenandoah Monday, and I can't carry it and the bread, too."

"Sorry, Jeannie-bean, I've got to get cleaned up and get out of these darned boots. And we're late as it is."

Sighing, she followed him into the house and deposited her straw bundle with its braided tail on the table. From the window Armel watched her go down the path, past Bronners' and Peron's and Jameses' houses. She angled across the grass and disappeared into the small brick bakery. The slight weight of guilt that he felt at making her go after the bread disappeared, too. Jeannie loved the bakery. And besides, she was ruining her eyes with all that braiding.

He turned and went through the parlor into his

small room behind it. While he changed the boots for his old soft moccasins handed down from Valmor and then Cabet, he felt the heady expansion that always came to him when he was alone in the house. After seventeen years of living with five other people in a sixteen-by-twenty foot cabin, the luxury of this house was still a delicious novelty. It had six rooms, with a glass window in each, smooth plank floors instead of unsteady puncheons, and no mud chinks falling out of the walls. Nothing leaked when it rained.

He sat for a moment on the edge of his bed and let his mind wander through the house, room by room. Two parlors downstairs side by side; two small behind-the-parlor bedrooms; two big bedrooms upstairs over the parlors; the narrow stairway that divided the house into equal units, a regular stairway, not a loft ladder.

Of course, he mused, if Cabet ever gets married, he and his wife will get the whole east half of the house. Jeannie'll have to give up her great big room over there and move back to this side of the house. But then, the way Cabet feels about girls, I guess there isn't much danger.

If Cabet doesn't get married, though, and I do, I wonder if I'll have to live over there. The thought was disturbing. It would be so much better to live in a separate house, preferably as far away from

Papa and Maman as possible.

An angry blast from the supper horn brought him to his feet. He splashed a little water on his face and arms and slammed out of the house.

CHAPTER TWO

Every face in the dining hall turned toward Armel as he moved among the tables toward his seat. The Duprees' table was on the far side, near a window and sheltered by the bulk of the spiral staircase. He smiled at Maman as he slid into his chair, and held up his clean damp hands to justify his lateness. She raised her eyebrows and let it pass.

From his table beside the serving pantry, President LeMan said loudly, "All right, Marie, you may start serving. We are finally all here." The dumbwaiter creaked in answer, and in a few moments Citizenne LeMan, Citizenne Hawbaker, and the two small Hawbakers were running food relays from the pantry to the tables.

Papa said, "Are you going to Meeting tonight?" Armel knew the question was for him; Cabet was twenty now, so it was mandatory that he attend the Saturday night meetings. Jeannie was not quite sixteen yet, so she was forbidden to attend. Only Armel, at seventeen, had a choice.

"I don't think so, Papa, if you'll ask about the Shenandoah trip for me. I can't sit still for that whole long meeting."

Papa reached for a slice of bread and began to spread it with Citizenne Bronner's strawberry preserve. "I assume then that you will be lurking around under a window somewhere, eavesdropping, during the meeting."

"I assume so." Armel's voice was an echo of Papa's courtroom tones. Their eyes met and smoldered for an instant; then Papa turned his attention to his bread.

As soon as possible after supper, Armel and Jeannie made their escape from the dining hall, along with the younger children. While Jeannie went home for her braiding straw, Armel sat on the dining hall step where he could get the last of the day's sun. Its warmth was barely strong enough to make itself felt, in competition with the evening coolness. Gooseflesh rose on his forearms below the rolled-back cuffs of his shirt.

On the grass between the dining hall and the south row of buildings all of Icaria's children were playing Ruth and Jacob, or it might have been Run, Sheep, Run—he couldn't tell for sure. Rolfe and Gretchen Hawbaker were there, and Emil and Louise Coteau, who were twelve and nine. Except for the Bettaniers' baby and Alexis James and Berthe Bronner, both of whom were older than Armel, this was the sum total of Icaria's younger generation.

From inside the dining hall behind him Armel could hear the scraping of tables and chairs as the room was made ready for the meeting. He could hear faint sounds of dishes being washed and put away, from the sloping wooden door beside him that led down into the basement-kitchen. Cabet was in the dining hall, and Alexis and Berthe. The others of his generation. He sighed, thinking he really should start going to Meeting instead of skulking around outside with the children. But it was a concession that he could not bring himself to make, at least not yet. Maybe if Papa wasn't always pushing . . .

34

Jeannie came out of the house with her straw bundle and started toward Armel, then veered back toward Catherine's cabin. A few minutes later she came carrying the tray with Catherine's empty supper dishes. She dropped her straw in Armel's lap and delivered the tray to the women downstairs.

By the time she came back, the meeting inside was being called to order. Armel stood up. "Come on. Let's go around back and sit under the window. We can hear better."

They settled on the grass beneath the window that was nearest the speakers, and leaned their backs against the clapboard flank of the building. Jeannie curled up, pulled her calico skirt in around her legs in absentminded modesty, and settled the straw bundle in her lap. Her hands started their supple work; the braid began to grow.

A gavel pounded. President LeMan called the meeting to order and began asking for committee reports.

Although Armel had said little to anyone these past few weeks about being allowed to go on the annual nursery-stock buying trip to Shenandoah, he was beginning to feel very strongly about it. Alexis had been allowed to go when he was Armel's age, and so had Cabet. If permission were denied him now, it would be a direct insult to his maturity. Sure, the trip was hard. They'd told him that often enough. But if permission were denied, he knew that the real, ground-bottom reason wouldn't be the hardships of the trip, or even, in all honesty, an insult to his manhood. The real reason would be President LeMan's reluctance to let boys or young men see how other people lived. At least that was what Valmor had told him years ago, before he left Icaria. And Valmor Dupree didn't lie, at least not to his little brother.

The committee reports were finished.

"The first order of business tonight is the Shenandoah trip." President LeMan's voice came loud and clear through the open window. Armel tensed.

"Citizen Bettanier, have you made your list?" Silence. "Will you read your list, please."

Bettanier's voice chanted, "Twenty flats of strawberries; four apple trees, preferably Jonathans, to replace the four that died last season; also I would like to suggest two peach trees and two apricot; and I guess that's all."

"Does anyone have any objections to Citizen Bettanier's list? Shall we vote? Yes, Citizen Bronner, what is it?"

"We need at least a dozen Osage orange plants to replace the parts of the pasture hedge that are dying."

A voice that sounded like Papa's rose. "I think we should quit wasting time and money on Osage orange hedges, and go ahead and build wooden fences around that pasture. We have plenty of timber down along the river. Those hedges are getting to the age where they're going to be dying out faster than we can replace them. They must be nearly eighteen years old; they were planted the first year or so we were here. There are already gaps in that hedge you could drive a hay wagon through."

"Oh, no," Armel whispered. "They're off on that old argument again. They'll be fighting over hedges versus fences all night."

"Maybe they won't," Jeannie the pacifier murmured.

Through the deepening dusk he watched the smooth weaving of her wrists over her braid of straw. It was almost totally dark now. The locusts in the woodlot were rasping in their dry rhythm. Suddenly three small figures burst around the corner. Rolfe Hawbaker scooted up to Armel and whispered, "Gretchen's 'It.' We're going to hide in the washhouse attic. Don't tell!" He was gone, streaking after the others toward the washhouse behind the bakery.

Armel and Jeannie exchanged glances of tolerant amusement. He wondered if she were wishing, too, that they weren't too old for a game of hide-and-go-seek in the intoxicating blackness of an April night.

Inside the hall Bronner was speaking again. ". . . sight of those hedges in the spring, when they're in full blossom. We mustn't be too eager to sacrifice beauty for utility. I think you'll all agree that hedges are more beautiful than any wooden fence ever thought of being."

A vote was taken; hedges won over fences, ten to five.

Now Papa will ask about my going along, thought Armel.

But President LeMan was off on another topic. "As you all know, when this dining hall was built many years ago, it was intended that Jean Fremont should put his considerable talent to work in painting the walls with murals of his own design. I recall quite vividly seeing his paintings on display in Paris many years ago, and I might say I have been eagerly awaiting the time when we could all be surrounded by works such as those. I believe the time has come when our treasury can bear the cost of the paints, and I further believe that these murals will be a significant step in the direction of our founder's dream of Icaria as a center of beauty and culture. Shall we vote?"

Armel sighed and moved to a more comfortable position against the clapboard ridges of the building. "They can think of more darned things to *vote* about," he growled.

"Shhh. They can hear you in there."

His attention was pulled sharply back to the meeting inside when he heard his name.

". . . help with the horses, and I think it's only fair, since Alexis and Cabet both went when they were Armel's age." It was Papa.

President LeMan said, "I don't know, Dupree. The boy has duties here. We can't let our youngsters run off all over the countryside on joy trips. What about it, Bronner?"

"I can get along without Armel for the week. I'll guard the breaks in the hedge myself if necessary. The boy deserves the trip. Besides, unless we let our young people see a little bit of the terrible ways that other people live, how can we expect them to appreciate Icaria?"

A low murmur began. Armel couldn't tell whether it was a murmur of assent or dissent. His jaw began to ache from its unconscious clenching. Even Jeannie became still as she strained to hear.

The discussion wandered off in the general direction of the wisdom, or unwisdom, of exposing young Icarians to outside influences. Eventually, though, it ran its course, and a vote was called for on the question of whether or not to allow Armel Dupree to accompany the older men to Shenandoah.

Together Armel and Jeannie stood up and looked over the windowsill into the room. The kerosene lanterns that lined the walls threw a soft, wavering light across the two rows of faces. The chairs were in a double semi-circle around the speaker's platform which was the slightly raised hearth in front of the fireplace.

"Those in favor of letting him go."

Most of the hands rose. Armel let out his breath and smiled.

"Those against."

Only three raised their hands—Fremont, Peron, and Ponte. They could usually be counted on to vote against the majority, no matter what the question was.

Jeannie grinned at him. "Good, you get to go. Let's go home now. My feet are getting wet in this dew."

Sunday breakfast was a late and leisurely affair. Armel and Bronner, Bettanier and Gentry, saw to the livestock in the minimal Sunday fashion and were cleaned up and ready for breakfast by the time the others began wandering across the grass toward the dining hall. The usual bread and butter and café au lait were supplemented this morning by flapjacks and apple cider.

As Armel and Cabet were leaving the dining hall, Alexis James caught up with them.

"How about setting out some prairie chicken

traps? We could take our guns along and pop off a few rabbits maybe."

Armel's glance caught Cabet's for an instant. Cabet wasn't any fonder of Alexis than Armel was, but he seldom went so far as to make excuses for not doing things with him, as Armel did constantly. Today, though, when Cabet agreed to the trapping, Armel allowed himself to be drawn in, too. His mind was so full of the trip to Shenandoah tomorrow that it seemed less trouble to go along than to come up with a plausible excuse.

It was an unusually fine morning. While Alexis and Cabet moved across the high open prairie beyond the east cornfield, Armel trailed several yards behind. Often he lost sight of them completely in the shallow hollows where the wild prairie grass was already waist high and where the prairie chickens hid. After a while he left the two of them and let his feet choose the direction they wanted to take. They went north, down the slope toward the bottomland and across the new Burlington and Missouri Railroad tracks. The tracks weren't so new really; they'd been there two years now, but they still seemed out of place in the Nodaway Valley.

When he came to the river, he pushed through the belt of trees and underbrush to the edge of the bank. It was a narrow river; even Rolfe could throw clods across it. But it was deep, and its green-brown water moved faster than it seemed.

Not too long now till we can swim, he thought, skipping a few pebbles downriver. Then he turned and began working his way back west toward the mills.

He could see them through the still-bare branches of the oaks and cottonwoods that lined the river. The gristmill was the smaller and closer of the two brick cubes. A well-worn ox road separated the mills and ended at the riverbank. As he passed the gristmill, Armel laid his hand for a moment on the small rough bricks. With some satisfaction he noticed that the ivylike vines he'd planted and trained were halfway up the wall and showing signs of coming to life again this year.

As he started up the ox road toward home, a train whistle sounded faintly from the direction of Corning, four miles to the west. He slowed his walk to an amble across the open bottomland, watching up the tracks for the train to appear around the hill. When he crossed the tracks, it hadn't come into sight yet, but the ground carried its vibrations. Walking backward, Armel climbed the steep slope toward home. On his right stretched the open sheep pasture; on his left the wooded hillside that provided Icaria with fuel.

The train was here now, suddenly filling the valley with its roar and screech and thunder. Armel waved; the fireman waved back.

When the caboose came into sight, he turned toward home. But, turning, he saw a figure standing on the brow of the hill in the pasture. It was a woman, with both arms raised, her fists clenched. White hair blew back from her face.

"Sacré gueulard!" Catherine screamed at the departing train. "Sacré gueulard!"

A smile pulled at Armel's mouth as he trudged on up the hill. But he found he really didn't want to laugh at the old woman shouting oaths at a railroad train. Something in the picture of Catherine disturbed him, and it continued to disturb him all through lunch.

After lunch he climbed the circular staircase to the library, meaning to stay just long enough to find something to take home. But by the time he found a book that he hadn't read recently, his escape was cut off. From the dining room downstairs came the whine of Berthe Bronner's violin, warming up.

He groaned. "Oh, no, another Musical Sunday." Rather than go down through the dining room and run the risk of Maman urging him to stay and enjoy the music, he curled up on the floor beneath the one small window and opened his book.

After a while the sky darkened and it began to rain. The music from downstairs was softened by the drumming of the rain on the roof, close over his head. When Gretchen Hawbaker and Louise Coteau sang "Alouette," their one duet, their tinny little-girls' voices barely reached the library.

Soon the sky outside became so dark with rain that there wasn't enough light to read by. Armel let his book fall shut and rolled over on his back, one arm across his eyes.

His thoughts turned to the buying trip. By this time tomorrow I'll be way on the other side of Corning. Maybe starting to look for a camping place for the night. I wonder if the prairie looks any different there. I wonder if Shenandoah is very much different from Corning. Bigger, probably. And the nurseries—wonder what they look like. Shenandoah probably has some lawyers. I might meet one—talk to him. What would it be like, living anyplace but Icaria. Just having one family, instead of a whole commune. Owning things all to yourself.

He frowned, straining to imagine life as it must be for hundreds of people. Not hundreds, thousands. Most of the rest of the world. Were they all wrong? Or were the Icarians . . .

His stomach was suddenly leaden. The trip loomed so large that he was unable to see past it to this time next week, when he'd be back in Icaria again and everything would be the same as before.

The rain drummed on. Slowly his arm fell away

from his face; one knee sagged over against the wall. Berthe's violin began a soft Viennese melody, but he didn't hear it.

Citizen Dupree left the dining hall with his wife after the music was finished. It was still an hour till supper, time enough for a nap maybe. Watching Jeannie walk ahead with the younger children, he thought, She's turning into a woman already. And that's the last of them. Armel and Cabet are men now. And Valmor . . .

But Valmor didn't count. Valmor was a traitor to Icaria, and no longer a son of Franz Dupree.

"I wonder where Armel's been all afternoon," Maman was saying. "He'd have enjoyed the music."

When her husband didn't answer, she slowed her pace and lowered her voice slightly. "Franz, you don't think there's any danger of Armel—getting ideas, do you, when he goes to Shenandoah? He's never really seen anything but what we have here. And Valmor—"

"Valmor was a fool. Armel is muleheaded, but he's not a fool. He won't be lured away from the life he knows is good and right just by one trip away from home."

Maman didn't say out loud that one trip was all it took to lure Valmor away, but the thought hung there between them.

They paused at their front door and turned to look back over the grassy square at the other couples and families moving toward their houses or standing and talking together. Dupree's arm dropped around his wife's shoulders.

"We have a good life here, Maman. Don't worry about Mel. He'll see the way other people live, and he'll never want to leave Icaria. He'll thank me for choosing this life for us."

She patted his hand on her shoulder. I'll believe him because I must believe him, she thought. I couldn't bear to lose two of my sons. Franz is right; he's always been right before. I just won't think ahead.

CHAPTER THREE

It was nearly sunset on Tuesday evening when President LeMan, walking beside the oxen, pointed his whip down the road and said, "There's Shenandoah."

From his seat atop one of the three mammoth Percherons, Armel squinted and looked, shading his eyes against the sun with his arm. From here, Shenandoah looked just like the three other towns they'd passed through, and all of them looked pretty much like Corning. A couple of mud roads, a half dozen frame buildings, and a scattering of tents, covered-wagon dwellings, sod houses, and tar-paper shacks, all set down any which way and connected by rambling footpaths.

The oxen and horses picked up speed now. The wagon creaked louder and jounced high on the rutted road. Jules Bettanier, leading one horse, kicked his mount into a trot, and Armel followed down the gentle slope into town.

On closer view he could see that Shenandoah was larger than he'd thought. Not so well settled and polished as Corning, but then Corning was a good fifty miles farther east and had been settled longer. There were two two-story hotels here, though, and five saloons and nearly as many stores of one kind or another.

"Armel, this way. We'll get the horses settled in the stable first thing." Jules motioned and Armel followed, feeling suddenly very much the country boy, bareback astride his Percheron. Too bad he and Jules weren't cantering in on well-bred saddle horses. Too bad President LeMan was with them. Jules was so young, even though he was a married man and a father, that tonight might have been fun with just the two of them.

His horse moved sideways to avoid two half-grown pigs. Then they were at the livery stable.

Feeling suddenly weary, Armel slid to the ground. He tried to hide the shakiness of his legs from the stableman who came to take the horses.

When LeMan drove in a few minutes later and made arrangements for the care of the horses and the ox team, the three men stood for a moment in the stable doorway. "Well," LeMan said finally, "let's go find a place to sleep." They turned and walked down the plank sidewalk.

Then Armel remembered the hats. He went back into the stable, to their wagon, and reached under the seat. There, carefully wrapped in prairie grass and tied in a gunnysack, were the twelve hats of braided wheat straw that were Jeannie's and Berthe's donation. He slung the deceptively light sack over one shoulder and loped to catch up with the others.

Jules and LeMan were waiting for him at the door of one of the hotels. They went in together. The lobby was a long dark room, lit by a few kerosene lanterns supplemented by an occasional wick-and-saucer lamp. The floors were planks, but in the center of the room was a large square linoleum rug, painted to look like Brussels carpet. Its colors fascinated Armel. Long trestle tables filled the room. Some twenty men sat around or on the tables, smoking and talking loudly.

"Dollar a night a head," said the woman seated at a small table near the door. "And you'll have to take dorm beds. Ain't got no rooms."

Nodding, President LeMan reached behind his beard and fished out the pouch that hung around his neck, the pouch that held the money allotted them from Icaria's treasury for the trip. With sudden interest Armel watched the transaction. It was the first he'd seen of money being given in exchange for something else, in this case for something as intangible as the privilege of sleeping for two nights in a building that belonged to someone, maybe to this woman.

The dorm beds proved to be mounds of prairie hay piled a foot thick on the floor, and arranged in a double row the length of the building, upstairs. There was just enough room between mounds for a man to stand and shed his clothes. The smell of sweat and unwashed bodies thickened the air.

Looking down at his bed, Armel decided to go outside and walk around for a while. Even though his muscles ached from two days on a broad-beamed horse, his mind was racing at such speed that he knew he would have to be much more tired before he could sleep. Besides, there wouldn't be much time tomorrow to explore on his own.

"President LeMan, would it be all right if I went out for a while? I'd like to have a look around."

LeMan was already stretched out on his hay bunk, his hands clasped over the money pouch under his beard. The hardened features, the hauteur of the man commanded respect even now, in his grayed and mended union suit. He opened his eyes and seemed to look directly into the deepest part of Armel's mind.

"You have no money, so there is no way you can be victimized. Yes. Go. Be back in an hour."

On an impulse Armel turned to Jules. "How about you? Want to come?"

Jules's mild round face brightened. His eyes sparkled for an instant, but glancing at President LeMan, he shook his head. The temptation to go with Armel to explore the town was outweighed by his wanting to ally himself with LeMan, who was already asleep. "You go ahead, Mel. Have a good time."

Outside the hotel, he breathed in the fresh night air and stood for several minutes pulling in the sounds and movement around him. The sky was dark to the east, but still pink and gold and blue to the west. Several people, mostly men, were moving about, crossing the deep-rutted street, calling to one another, dodging horses, dogs, stray pigs, and each other. There was an air of celebration. Armel tried to pinpoint it, and finally decided it must just seem that way to him because the only times he'd ever been in a town were the Fourth of July's in Corning.

He started up the plank sidewalk in the direction of the setting sun. When people smiled or nodded at him, he returned their smiles and walked a shade taller. Gradually his tiny fears of being set apart from the townspeople, maybe even looked down on, began to fade. A woman and a girl walked by, hurrying toward some destination or other; the girl glanced with quick appraisal at Armel. The appraisal ended at his eyes, and he felt her interest. It kindled him. Back home there was no one to look at him that way.

He went on, past the open door of one of the saloons. It looked inviting in there, with the piano playing and everyone laughing and shouting back and forth—and girls. But he was pretty sure you had to have money to spend before you could go into those places. And, of course, he was Icarian . . .

At the end of the street he crossed over and started back on the other side. Suddenly a lighted window caught his eye. On the glass were the words "John Mason, Attorney at Law, Notary Public." Without thinking, Armel moved closer until he was staring into the room. It was a tiny place, just big enough for a cluttered rolltop desk and a huge chair, one stack of books and another of papers and folders. A young man sat behind the desk, leaning on his elbows and studying a long sheet of paper. There was a gold seal on a bottom corner of the paper, and Armel could see signatures in the other corner. The man wore a white shirt with sleeve garters and a narrow black string tie. His vest was maroon paisley

—like Catherine's shawl, Armel thought, smiling—
and his trousers were black and very neat.

For more than fifteen minutes Armel stood in
the darkness outside the window, staring at the man.
As he looked, the figure at the desk faded, became
Armel, an Armel who did the work he wanted to do,
who lived in a house in town and had a wife—the girl
on the sidewalk just now—a man who owned things.
A horse that belonged to him alone. His clothes,
picked out by him and paid for by him with money
he had earned by being the most brilliant lawyer in
the county. And was it really so impossible? Hadn't
Papa been just exactly like that, years ago in France?
A brilliant young lawyer who lived with his wife in
his own house and rode his own horse and bought
his own clothes.

But Papa had given all that up for Icaria. So
evidently Icaria was better than this. If it weren't,
Papa certainly would never have chosen it. There
must be something wrong with living like this, with
owning things and doing what you want with your
life. The evil must be hidden somewhere—behind
the glass of the window, inside the houses and stores
of this town, inside the people.

He turned abruptly, as if he could see the evil by
looking quickly before it had a chance to hide itself.
A man, passing on the sidewalk behind him, nodded
and touched his hat.

With one last long look at John Mason, Attorney at Law and Notary Public, Armel went on his way. He moved slowly down the walk, looking into the cluttered windows of a general store, peering into the open doors of another saloon, nodding and smiling.

At the end of the block, where the plank sidewalk dissolved to a mud path, he paused. Ahead of him was a long, low-roofed shed that stretched away into the dark between broad, flat plots where row upon row of young plants grew. The sign above the front door, barely legible in the dusk, said "Shenandoah Nurseries, E. Grask, Prop."

This was the nursery, then. Armel jumped down off the end of the sidewalk and walked closer. The first rows appeared to be poplar trees, all under two feet high. A few rows beyond the poplars were the Osage orange seedlings, and beyond them a few rows of twiggy lilac bushes, some with tiny clusters of buds just beginning to show color. He dropped to his knees to read the tag on one of the bushes. "Persian Lilac," it said. There had been lilacs around a few of the cabins at home, but they'd all died off a few years ago. He leaned closer, seeking the half-remembered scent of the blossoms.

"Anything I can help you with, young man?"

With a guilty start he straightened up. The man on the other side of the lilac row was shorter than

54

Armel, squarely built, clean-shaven. His face was only a shadow beneath his felt hat, but his stance, his voice, were friendly.

"I beg your pardon. I was just—"

"Sorry, son, you'll have to talk English, I'm afraid."

Armel flushed. He'd forgotten he was speaking in the more familiar French. He spoke more slowly, trying to remember his English lessons and translating in his mind as he went. "I'm sorry to intrude. I was just admiring the *fleurs*—the flowers. I haven't seen any lilacs for some time."

The shadow smiled. "You must be one of them Icarians, aren't you. Figured some of you folks would be coming in one of these days."

Armel nodded.

"Ed Grask." The man stuck out his hand.

Armel shook it and replied, "Armel Dupree, sir. This is your nursery, then?"

"All mine, lock and stock, as they say." Grask turned to look over his shoulder at the rows of seedlings and young trees, etched by moonlight.

Armel looked at them, too. It must be a strange feeling—a glorious, powerful feeling—to be able to look at a plot of land, a building, a hundred baby trees, and say, "This is all mine." A feeling he would never know. A tiny ache that had been born a few minutes ago outside the lawyer's office window—or had it been born long before that—began to make itself felt in the pit of his stomach. There was something in life, something big and good, that other people had and that he could not have because he was Icarian.

"If you want to look at flowers, Arnold, come in here a minute." The man turned and walked toward the shed. Armel followed, not bothering to correct the name.

Inside the shed they lit lanterns and walked the seemingly endless length of the building, pausing at the wooden tables and racks that lined the walk while Grask explained about each group of plants. Most of the names, especially those of the flowers, were unfamiliar to Armel, but he nodded and admired and examined with great enthusiasm.

One tabletop was covered with small square compartments. Each compartment held several tiny paper packets, and each packet had written across it the name of the seeds inside. Armel picked up one packet and read "Watermelon."

"You folks have any watermelons back home?" Grask said.

Armel shook his head. "I think we might have had some a long time ago. Are they about so big, and yellow in the middle?"

"No, you're thinking of muskmelons. Watermelons are, oh, *this* big, green on the outside and red inside with black seeds."

"Oh, yes!" Armel grinned suddenly. "We had some in Corning one year at Fourth of July. I ate so much I got sick. It was the best thing I'd ever tasted."

Grask winked and nodded toward the packet still in Armel's hands. "You better buy a few of those seeds, then, and get you a patch going at home. Nothing better than good cold watermelon on a summer day. Only ten cents for two dozen seeds."

Ten cents. Such a small amount. It might as well have been a million cents, though. Flushing in the dim light of the lantern, Armel shook his head and put the packet back.

"Oh, I forgot. They don't let you have any money of your own, do they? Tell you what—you just take those seeds along, Arnold. Ain't no boy should be without watermelons. Just don't you tell the others, and you can have them all to yourself."

Armel looked from the seeds to the man's face. His first instinct had been to defend Icaria against this man's remark. His next reaction was to take the seeds and thank him, which he did. His third reaction, delayed until he was outside again on his way to the hotel, was wonder and envy. That man back there, standing in the middle of his very own building and land, had the ability to do something that Armel had never done—and would never be able to do. He had given a gift. He owned things, and therefore, if he found a boy looking at his lilac plants one April evening, and liked the boy and wanted to give him some small thing, he could. It was as simple as that.

Suddenly the small brown packet in his hand became the most important thing in his existence. It belonged to him. Just him. Armel Dupree. No one in Icaria knew about it. These seeds were his to plant and take care of, or to give away if he felt like it, or to throw away even. He owned them.

"Hey there, old sow, what do you think about *that?*" A large white sow, rooting in the mud beside the walk, looked up at him for a brief moment, blinked her small eyes, and went back to her rooting.

When Armel had picked his way among the pallet-beds in the dorm room and found his own beside President LeMan, and had pulled off his boots and stretched out, the packet of seeds was tucked away out of sight inside his union suit. He fell into a deep, motionless sleep and dreamed about Valmor as he had been just before he went away.

CHAPTER FOUR

Next morning the three Icarians ate breakfast in the dining room below the dorm, with some forty other travelers and businessmen. To Armel it was a harsh and unsavory meal. There was black American coffee instead of the creamy café au lait he was used to, and corn mush with the taste and consistency of paste. But the small packet scratching lightly against his ribs under his shirt made up for the poor food.

After their breakfasts were eaten and paid for from the pouch under LeMan's beard, they went out into the morning sun and across the street to the general store Armel had looked into last night. The street was alive this morning with horse- or ox-drawn wagons, pedestrians, and the ever-present stray animals. Daylight somewhat diminished the holiday air, though, or perhaps it was just that now there was business to attend to.

In the general store President LeMan offered up the gunnysack that held the girls' straw hats. While Armel watched from a little distance, his eyes following every move of the transaction, the man behind the counter examined a few of the hats, nodded, mentioned a price. LeMan stroked the broad fall of beard that covered his chest. He nodded too, but stipulated that the money would have to be in hard coin, not that questionable paper money. Coins were dropped into his hand; all of the hats were pulled out of their prairie hay nests, brushed off, and set out on a long trestle table with bins of ribbons and bolts of linsey-woolsey.

By then it was ten o'clock, time to meet the man who was buying the horses. He was waiting for them at the livery stable, a tall, emaciated man in loose-hanging striped coveralls. One by one the Percherons were led out into the sunlight to be examined from all angles, prodded and tested, gaited up and down the road with Armel or Jules at their halters. By the time the buyer was convinced of the horses' soundness, and his bank draft was tucked into LeMan's pouch, it was close to noon.

After lunch in the hotel the three of them walked the length of the street to where their main business waited, the buying of the nursery stock.

Mr. Grask was waiting just outside the long shed. He and LeMan shook hands. Then LeMan indicated the others. "This is our Crops Chief, Jules Bettanier." More handshaking. "And one of our younger members, Armel Dupree."

For an instant Armel hesitated between acknowledging the introduction and saying they'd already met. But Mr. Grask, looking directly at Armel and slightly away from the others, smiled, and hidden in the folds of the smile was a wink.

"Howdy' do, Mr. Dupree. Glad to know you." The handshake ended with a small quick pressure; the packet of watermelon seeds made itself felt against his skin. Gravely Armel nodded. "Pleasure, Mr. Grask."

After an hour or so of standing among rows of Osage orange seedlings while Jules examined and discarded, Armel excused himself, saying he would meet them at the hotel at suppertime.

As he moved slowly along the warped boards of the sidewalk, he was restlessly aware that these few hours would be the last he'd have, possibly for years, in which to taste this way of life. There was something here, something good enough to have pulled Valmor away from Icaria even though he'd known what his leaving would do to Maman, something bad enough to have made the citizens of Icaria and all who had died along the way to Iowa from France leave homes and families and occupations and established ways of life. What was there about the way the rest of the world lived that Papa, in his unquestionable wisdom, wanted to shield his family from?

Hands in his pants pockets, eyes darting, Armel made his way up the street, back down the other side, then along the paths and wagon tracks that led among the dwellings. Most of the houses were worse than Icaria's best; few were worse than Icaria's worst had been a few years ago. Some of them were far better than Icaria could ever aspire to—large square frame houses with porches and bay windows and small private barns out back. There were only three or four of these, on the far edge of town, but Armel had the feeling that, inevitably, the tar-paper shacks, the tents and sod houses and covered wagons would be replaced with houses like these—houses where a man like John Mason, Attorney at Law and Notary Public, might live.

Abruptly he turned and made his way back to the street where the stores were. I can't find out anything by looking in windows, he decided. I'm going to have to talk to someone. If he's in his office and not busy, maybe I'll just go in and tell him— I'll tell him I'm interested in becoming a lawyer. That should do to start a conversation.

He was in luck. John Mason was sitting outside his office on the edge of the wooden sidewalk, shredding a blade of grass with his thumbnail.

Reminding himself to speak English, Armel said, "Pardon, could you spare me a few moments? I'd like to ask your advice."

The young man looked up over his shoulder. "By all means. Can we sit out here and enjoy the sunshine while we talk, or would you rather go inside and be private?"

Armel answered by dropping to the sun-warmed planks and picking himself a blade of grass from between his feet. "I'm Armel Dupree, from over near Corning, and I—"

"Glad to meet you. John Mason from Muscatine." They shook hands.

"I was wondering if you could tell me how I should go about becoming a lawyer." The question that had begun as nothing more than a conversation-starter took on a quality of truth that surprised Armel for an instant, when he heard the words spoken. Then, oddly, they became something that he had felt for a long time, but had never acknowledged to himself.

Mason was looking at him in much the same way that the farmer had looked at the three Percherons that morning. "How old are you, and what have you done so far along these lines?"

"I'm seventeen, and all I've had a chance to do so far is to read my father's law books."

"Your father is a lawyer? Does he practice in Corning?"

Suddenly Armel felt reluctant to mention Icaria. "No, we farm now. But he was a lawyer back in France, before I was born. A famous trial lawyer."

"Dupree, Dupree . . ." Mason's eyes wandered off. He frowned, struggling for recollection. "I think I've heard of him. Wasn't there some sort of—trouble—maybe, oh, twenty years ago or longer? I'm just sure I remember studying a case—"

"Of course there wasn't any trouble," Armel flared. "Papa was one of the best lawyers in France. He only gave it up because he believed in—" He bit off his sentence.

Mason was looking at Armel again, studying his face with friendly interest. "You're one of those Icarians, aren't you? I've heard about your communist settlement over there, and it's always fascinated me. Tell me. Just how much freedom do you folks have—as individuals, I mean? I hope you don't mind my asking."

The question was asked in such a clinical way that Armel found himself answering in the same spirit. He dug one heel into the dust of the road and ground it thoughtfully.

"Well, let's see. Freedom . . ." It was a hard question. He'd never really stopped to analyze that aspect of Icaria.

Mason prompted gently. "I've heard that somebody, your leader or a committee or somebody, tells you what your profession will be. And they tell you when you have to get married, and to whom. Is that right?"

"Our President doesn't have any real power at all. Everybody votes on things." He thought a moment. "I don't know for sure about the marriage part. I guess they could decide that for a person. I don't remember the question ever coming up before."

He thought back. Jules Bettanier's wedding was the only one he could recall within Icaria, and as far as Armel knew, there had never been any question in anyone's mind but that Jules and Marie would get married. Valmor had been only seventeen when he left, and now that he thought about it, the other young men had either left Icaria as soon as they were out of school or had stayed unmarried, like Cabet and Alexis, and Peron and Ponte and Fremont. The girls must have left, too, he realized with a start. There was just Berthe now, and of course Jeannie and the youngsters. The thought made his stomach suddenly tighten.

He veered in another direction. "About the pro-

fessions, the commune takes a vote when a person
gets to be sixteen and too old for school. They
assign him whatever job they think he can do for
the greatest good of Icaria." The statement sounded
like just what it was, an echoing of Papa and Citizen
Bronner.

"This is all very interesting," Mason mused.
"And what have they assigned you to do for the
greatest good of Icaria?"

Armel's heel dug diligently. "Assistant to the
Small Stock Chairman."

"Beg pardon, I didn't quite hear you."

"I help with the sheep!" Armel was intensely
annoyed with the direction the conversation was
taking.

"And in your free time, when you're not assist-
ing the Small Stock Chairman, you read your
father's law books." There was a long silence. "Tell
me, Mr. Dupree, just what is the essence of the
Icarian ideology? Why is your way of doing things
superior to other people's?"

Armel's chest expanded as he drew a long
breath. Here was a question he could answer.
Forgotten for the moment were his own awakening
doubts about all the things that had made up his
life until now.

"We believe," he recited, "that if the common
good is put above individual gain, everyone will

66

benefit. All property is owned by the commune, and everyone's needs are taken care of from the common stock. All our profits go into one fund, and that fund feeds and clothes all of us. That way, no one has any more than anyone else, so there is no greed, no theft, no crimes of any kind. All are equal, and all are treated equally."

There was another long silence. Then Mason said, very quietly, "*Are* you all really equal? I mean, aren't there some that are willing just to go mindlessly along, take what they're given, let the commune worry about everything for them?"

Armel was immediately defensive, but while he paused to put out of his mind the picture of four men standing under a tree while he and Bronner chased the community hens in the rain, Mason went on.

"I may be wrong about this, but I've thought about it sometimes, and it seems to me that a man who started out to be hardworking, ambitious, maybe even talented in some way or another, would end up doing the same bare minimum of work that the lazy, stupid man did, because—why not? I should think it would have a corrosive effect on a person after a while."

Armel reddened. He wanted to come back with a sharp, decisive answer, but he was suddenly confused. His mind couldn't quite focus on the question, and he couldn't marshall the logical arguments that he knew existed. What would Papa have said?

"I'm sorry," Mason said abruptly. "I've been rude, I'm afraid, talking down a way of life that I know nothing about. Would you like to come in and look around my office? I think I may have some literature I could give you that would explain the Iowa laws for legal training and admittance to the bar. Just in case you should ever need an attorney in Icaria."

Eagerly Armel rose and followed him inside.

Early the next morning the three Icarians started home. It was slower going now, because the wagon was piled high with nursery stock, so high there was no room for riders. LeMan walked beside the oxen, where he could prod when necessary. Jules Bettanier led the way, watching for bogs in the road and waving to occasional travelers or to farmers hacking their small fields from the matted roots of the prairie grass.

Armel followed some distance behind the wagon. He didn't see the red-winged blackbirds that perched on dipping stalks of grass and watched him pass. He didn't see the rabbits nor the gaudy pheasants nor the deer that sailed over the low hills. A prairie rattler slid off the road into the grass almost under his feet.

He set his course directly between the double tracks of the road, where the grass was short enough to make the walking easy. His mind, freed from the necessity of guiding his feet, was at work assimilating his impressions of Shenandoah. All those people—probably close to five hundred of them—multiplied by all the other towns in Iowa, in the whole country. Not to mention all the farms in between. All those people lived lives as different from his as—his mind searched for a simile, and failed.

Were all those people really wrong? Or could it be that Papa was wrong, and Bronner and LeMan and all of them, including himself? It seemed unlikely. Papa was a brilliant man. So was Bronner, or at least he *had* been when he was a professor back in France. And what about Fremont? He was a well-known artist, almost famous. He wouldn't have given up a career like that to join the Icarians if he hadn't believed this was the best way to live. And the same with Papa.

He frowned suddenly. Something he'd just thought of, or almost thought of, bothered him. Something was not right, but when he searched back through his line of thought, the disturbing shadow recoiled and refused to be identified.

So he thought instead about the two things inside his shirt. The watermelon seeds—where would be the best place to plant them? Someplace where no one would find them. And then, when the melons were ripe, he could surprise everybody. Or maybe he'd hoard them, eat them all himself. If no one else knew about them, no one would feel bad at having missed them.

It occurred to him that keeping the melons a secret would be considered wrong by President Le-Man and some of the others, possibly even Papa. What would they do to him if they found out? Quickly he shrugged the question aside. Surely no one would mind very much about a few water-melons, he told himself, turning his thoughts to the other item inside his shirt.

The pamphlet—*Requirements for Entering the Bar, State of Iowa.* The second gift of his lifetime, given to him by an almost total stranger, as were the watermelon seeds.

He sighed. It sure must be a good feeling to own something, to want to give it to someone—and to be able to.

A sudden thought brought him to a standstill. In a few months, when the melons are ripe, *I'll* have something I can give away. But who shall I give them to? Divide them up among everyone? No, that's what I'd be expected to do. That's what we've always had to do with everything. Maman! Sure, she's the one I'd most like to give a present to. He began walking again, smiling to himself as he pictured Maman's face when he lugged home his crop of huge green melons. They'd have a family feast. A private family feast, just the five of them . . .

"Armel, lend a hand here."

He looked up from his thoughts, and groaned. The wagon was stuck again, hub deep in black mire. Berry and Boss were straining into their yokes, their muzzles nearly touching the ground. Jules was waving his arms and apologizing for misjudging the depth of the mud, and LeMan was pulling the pry-poles down from the wagon with heavy patience. In the end, they had to unload the hedge seedlings, the strawberry flats, the slender apple trees, and the peach and apricot trees before the lightened wagon could be pulled and pried from the mire.

They made fifteen miles that day and spent the night at the same farm, near Nyman, that they'd stayed at on the way down. Next day they covered another fifteen miles northeast and forded the west branch of the Nodaway just south of Villisca. By late afternoon of the following day they were fording their own east branch of the Nodaway at the good shale-bottom ford at Corning. After a few miles more, there were the outlying wheat fields of Icaria, then the schoolhouse, the cornfields and vineyards, and finally the trees and roofs of home.

Armel was leading the way now, straining for the first sight of his world, straining for the reassurance that it was, as it had always been for him, the only place that actually existed. The only place where things were as they should be.

The windows in the dining hall were lit; the meeting was going on inside. Around the dining hall, the brood of houses and shops were blocky shadows in the twilight. Everything was in order.

But then why did it seem—distorted—as though he were seeing the commune reflected in the river water? It was just as it had always been. It was home. Wasn't it?

CHAPTER FIVE

Armel woke the next morning to the sound of some-
one kicking lightly against his bedroom door. Ah,
Sunday morning, he thought, stretching and smiling.
A whole day with nothing I have to do!

"Mel, I brought your breakfast."

He leaned out of bed, across the narrow space
of the room, and pulled the door open. The dinner
tray usually reserved for Catherine's meals teetered

in Jeannie's hands as she came through the doorway.

"Sit up now, and you can eat this in bed. Maman thought you should rest up from your trip." She settled the tray over his knees. "Catherine was mad as a stuck pig that she had to go to the dining hall to eat so you could use her tray."

Beneath the tray and the calico comforter, Armel's legs ached with a weariness made pleasant by knowing he didn't have to get up. He stretched again, yawned mightily, and made a gleeful face at the food on the tray.

Jeannie sat on the foot of his bed, her back propped against the back wall, as if she were settling in for a long visit. But she was oddly quiet. Finally, in a making-conversation tone, she said, "Well, tell me all about the trip. How did you like it in Shenandoah?"

He set down his café cup and buttered a slice of bread. "I told you all about it already." The family had sat up for an hour after Meeting the night before, asking polite questions about his trip. Now that he thought about it, Jeannie had been awfully quiet last night, too.

He watched her now. She was tracing the comforter pattern with one finger, not looking at him.

"All right, Jeannie. What are you in mourning about?"

"Nothing."

"Come on. I know you want to talk about it.

Something happen while I was gone?"

"Oh, it's just—I was kind of disappointed. They voted on me at Meeting last night."

He stopped chewing to think. Oh, sure. He had missed Jeannie's birthday last week. She was sixteen now. Her schooldays were over. "What did they decide?"

She hugged her legs and rested her chin on her kneecaps, so that her words came out between clenched teeth. "Washhouse."

"Oh." Washhouse duty for Jeannie the rest of her life, unless the voters decided she was needed more somewhere else. The washhouse, with its unbearable steam in the summer, the tubs of scalding water, the lye soap . . . He glanced at the fine peach skin of her hands. "You were hoping for the bakery, weren't you?"

She nodded as best she could, with her knees in the way of her chin.

"Did you tell them you wanted to work there?"

She nodded again. "They have all the help they need in the bakery, and Citizenne Coteau's been all alone in the washhouse since Citizenne Gentry died."

She sounded so resigned, so placid about the decision that Armel was suddenly irritated at her. He remembered how he'd hated it when they voted him into the sheep-watching business over a year ago. He'd argued with Papa all night, insisting that he'd be wasted watching sheep for the rest of his life.

But of course that was the area where help was needed, and arguing with Papa, and with the President later, had been futile. And maybe they'd been right. The past year and a half hadn't been too bad. At least it hadn't *seemed* so bad until . . .

But here sat Jeannie, calmly accepting her life sentence to the washhouse with no more protest than a few sighs.

"Jeannie, do you ever think about . . . I mean, do you ever wonder whether . . . Are you sure, deep down, that this"—he waved toward the window and the commune outside—"is right? I mean, there are a great many people in the world who don't live the way we do. How do we know for sure that they're not right, and we're wrong?"

She picked her head up from her knees and turned it slowly toward him. Expressions, like shadows, moved across it; she was startled, then alarmed.

"Mel, don't talk that way! You sound just like—"

"Just like Valmor did when he came back from his first trip away from home? Before he decided that maybe it was Icaria that was out of step, instead of the rest of the world?"

They stared at each other, her eyes searching his face, while his gradually lost their belligerence.

Finally she said, "You don't really feel that way, do you? It would just about kill Maman if you wanted to go away, too."

He felt suddenly helpless. The tray across his knees was a trap. Maman's love was a trap, and so was Papa's unquestionable wisdom that left no room for logical argument, especially about Icaria.

As if she'd read his thoughts, she said, "Icaria is the one perfect society. You know that. Papa wouldn't have given up all he had back in France otherwise. And you know Maman loves it here. And so do I, and Cabet, and you did too. Just because I got assigned to the washhouse doesn't change anything. That's where I'm needed for the good of the commune, so that's where I'll go."

Good little docile Icarian, he thought wryly.

From the front of the house came a sudden call, high and querulous. "Jeanne Marie Dupree!"

Jeannie glanced at Armel and made a face. "Old Catherine. I wish she'd knock, like everyone else." She got down from the bed and left the room.

Chewing more slowly so that he could hear better, Armel listened to the exchange at the door.

"You tell your maman I want my paisley shawl back. Your maman isn't my friend. She has no more respect for a sick old lady . . ." The rest was lost in muttering.

Jeannie's voice was so low he caught only an

occasional word. ". . . does respect you . . . misunderstanding, I'm sure . . . get it for you if you want . . ."

She left Catherine at the door while she ran upstairs to her parents' room to get the shawl. When she'd given it to Catherine and closed the door, she scurried back to kneel at Armel's window. "Who do you think she's going to give it to now?"

Setting aside the empty tray, Armel joined her at the window, keeping low in case Catherine should look back and see them spying on her. The old woman's back was rigid as buckram, her step firm, as she crossed the deserted square. When she was out of sight from Armel's window, they moved to the front room to watch from there.

At Fremont's cabin, straight across from the Duprees', she slowed to her accustomed bent hobble and stopped outside the door. The pantomime that followed was as clear to Jeannie and Armel as though they could hear Catherine's words. In a few minutes the paisley shawl and Catherine's undying friendship were offered to Citizen Fremont, and accepted.

Then Papa and Maman were home from breakfast, and the chance was gone to try to find out what Jeannie honestly felt about Icaria.

The important thing today, he thought as he went back into his room, is to get the watermelons planted. He skimmed out of his union suit, for the first time in a week, and tossed it in a corner with the pants and shirt that also had been on him for a week. As he pulled on his other union suit, it occurred to him that from now on Jeannie was going to be laundering his underwear—and that of everyone else in Icaria. The idea was distasteful.

The thought of the washhouse reminded him that, except for the times he'd been caught in the rain recently, it had been quite a while since he had actually bathed. He took down his soft old denim Amana blues from their wall peg and stepped into them. Then, carrying his boots, he left the house and walked barefoot up the path past Bronners' house, around the back of the bakery, to the washhouse that sat in the shade of the dining hall. From the well beside the washhouse door he pulled up bucket after bucket of water, carried them inside, and poured them into one of the tin-lined washtubs. He smiled, thinking how the bath business had picked up this last year, since the well was dug. Before, it had been a quarter-mile walk, all uphill, to haul water from the river.

He hung the little bark "Stay Out" sign on the door, pulled it shut, and eased himself into the icy water. A few minutes later he emerged, clean and nearly numb.

Back in his room, with the door tight shut, he

lifted the end of the comforter at the foot of his bed and untied the twine that held the mattress closed. He reached into the mattress sack, felt through the tight-packed prairie hay, and finally found the packet of seeds. He made sure the pamphlet was still in there, too, before he withdrew his arm and retied the twine.

Planting directions were penned faintly on the back of the packet. Plant in sandy loam, it said, preferably near a river or stream. Six seeds to a hill, hills ten feet apart. Plenty of sun.

He slipped the packet inside his shirt and eased past Maman in the front room. She started to ask where he was going, but he was gone before she got the question out. He loped around the house and into the dense green-black of the woodlot. The stand of oak and hickory and elms covered more than twenty acres, the entire area bounded by the commune, the railroad track at the foot of the hill, the mill road to the east, and the truck farm and orchard to the west of the commune.

As he made his way down the slope, over tree roots and around clumps of brush, his mind went over every part of the Icarian land. The places best for the watermelons were all places where someone was bound to find them. The riverbank near the mills was too heavily wooded. West of the woods, the cornfield ran up to within a few yards of the river. The men working in the fields would be sure to see anything as big as a watermelon. East of the mills it was the same problem.

He kept thinking, Sandy loam—by the river—lots of sun. The glare of sunlight on the railroad tracks below caught his eye, and his attention. The trestle. Of course. He was running now, plunging down the slope and out of the woods into the sun. He veered left at the tracks and forced himself down to a walk, in case anyone should be watching. Whistling softly under his breath, he stepped up onto the rail and walked it, arms raised, in perfect balance.

At the western boundary of the Icarian land the river curved south and slipped under a single-track trestle. Armel glanced casually right and left, then even more casually back over his shoulder. No one in sight. He slid down the incline to the river's edge. There, under the trestle, was a sloping patch of sandy soil, striped with sun and the shade of the ties overhead.

"Not 'full sun' for you, watermelon seeds, but it's safer this way." He spoke quietly as he opened the packet and poured the oval seeds out on the ground.

The seed hills couldn't be ten feet apart, either. There wasn't room. But he spaced the four sand mounds as far apart as possible, and tucked six seeds into each. Then he tore the packet into small pieces and tossed them out onto the river. "There. That's done." Looking out carefully first, he climbed the embankment and started home.

Not far from the edge of the woodlot, where it neared the back of the bakery, he noticed an arrangement of twigs on the ground, almost beneath his feet. Smiling, he dropped to the ground beside it. A tiny twig fence, three inches high and roughly a foot square, marked the boundaries of a caterpillar corral. More twigs inside the fence formed a crude house. A handful of grass, roots and all, lay against one side of the fence as food for the caterpillar. A flat pebble with a shallow depression held drinking water.

Armel smiled. Gretchen Hawbaker and Louise Coteau, probably. They were the only ones now who were at the caterpillar-house age. He looked up, expecting to see two pairs of eyes watching him from behind, or in, a tree. But the builders of the property weren't in sight.

He noticed they had picked a handful of violets for the caterpillar. The flowers were leaning against the twig house, their threadlike stems already dried, their blossoms drooping.

He reached in to pick up the violets, and in doing so uncovered the recipient of all this loving care. It was what Armel and Jeannie had always called a brown-bear caterpillar, with fur half an inch long. It was divided into exact thirds, the front and the back third a rich russet and the middle third black. It was curled into a tight, miserable ball.

As he sat watching the caterpillar, Armel's high spirits faded. There was something unsettling about the way the caterpillar ceased to function inside its prison even though Gretchen and Louise had obviously worked hard to provide it with everything it needed, and even though the girls hadn't *meant* it to be a prison, but rather a place where their caterpillar could live better than all other caterpillars.

Frowning suddenly, Armel picked up the caterpillar, ran his fingertips over the soft bristles of its fur, and set it on the lowest branch of the tree overhead. Then, feeling somewhat better and somewhat worse, he went home. After lunch he shut himself in his room and read the pamphlet on the Iowa laws for bar examinations.

CHAPTER SIX

"Get in there, old girl." Armel swatted the gray woolly rear of the last ewe to plod into the sheep pen. He wired the gate shut and glanced across the road toward the dining hall. People haven't started coming to supper yet, he thought. I probably have time to stop at Fremont's.

As he started up the road, he saw something out of place, dark moving shapes in the cornfield behind the barns. Cows. A dozen or so of them, meandering through the fragile shoots of corn, crushing the baby stalks with their hooves.

He was already running toward them when he saw the men lounging in the shade of the horse barn. Alexis James, Peron, and Ponte. Armel's mind registered their names automatically, and even as he shouted at them, he knew how they were going to respond.

"Hey. Give me a hand, will you? The cows are out. They're in the corn."

Three heads turned toward him. One set of shoulders shrugged. The men went on with their conversation.

Anger halted him. He clenched his fists and searched for searing words that would penetrate their stupid indifference. But the futility of arguing with them and the necessity of catching the cows before the whole field was trampled, moved him into action again.

It was frustrating work, getting the widely scattered and perfectly contented cows headed back to their pasture, but finally the last of them strolled through the break in the hedge, nodding her head and swinging a small cornstalk between her teeth in rhythm with her gait. He found a branch blown down from a dead tree, and fixed it as best he could across the gap in the hedge.

By the time he got back across the road Alexis and the others were out of sight.

They're probably waiting at the dining hall, so they'll be first in line for supper, he grumbled to himself. And I've probably missed another chance to get Fremont to fix these blasted boots.

The thought reminded him of how uncomfortable his toes were in the tight shoes. He began to hobble a little. A vague despondency appeared out of nowhere and began to follow him. Maybe it was caused by the boots, or the stupidity of those three clods standing around while the cows ruined the corn, or Bronner's insistence on the decorative but impractical hedges. Or maybe he was depressed because everything was just the same as it had always been, and probably would always be. The Shenandoah trip was a month-old memory, and its effects were beginning to wear off. What good did it do, anyway, to compare Icaria with the rest of the world? This was where he was.

As he passed the log cabin that served as Citizen Fremont's manufactory of boots, shoes, saddles, and harness, he noticed the door standing open and went inside.

The front room of the cabin was a welter of brown and black shadows that the sunlight behind Armel failed to penetrate. Tangled heaps of harness filled the corners. The floor was covered with scraps and curling peels of leather. The window was grimy and curtained with cobwebs. Dust was thick everywhere except in the narrow path from the front door to the curtained entrance to the back room.

"Citizen Fremont, are you here?"

From behind the curtain came a surly voice. "Yes, what do you want?"

Armel pulled the curtain aside but didn't go past the doorway. No one went into Jean Fremont's back room unless he was definitely invited, and Fremont never invited.

The back room was as bright and spotless as a man could make it, in startling contrast to the shop room. The walls were whitewashed, the floors covered with red and green rag rugs, the windows curtained with green gingham. A gay quilt covered the bed in one corner, and gleaming copper pots on the chest held arrangements of dried wild flowers. And yet the room had an element of starkness that bothered Armel until he pinpointed it. There were no pictures to relieve the blank whiteness of the walls.

Fremont stood near the door, ready to defend his sanctuary from Armel's eyes. His face was long and fine-featured, with skin like age-grayed wood. Sparse brown hair stood out from a receding forehead. His lips had an indefinable softness that Armel had always found faintly repugnant.

"Well, what is it you want here?" Fremont thrust his head forward from his shoulders, rounded almost to the point of deformity.

Armel started to tell him, then stopped when he saw the drawings stacked neatly on the small table under the window. He glanced at Fremont. The long face, never expressionless, was wavering now between a fierce defense of his privacy and a tentative eagerness to show off his drawings. Fremont stooped and picked up the mammoth tiger-striped tomcat standing against his leg. It settled on the soft paunch of his stomach.

Armel nodded toward the drawings. "May I look at them? Are they the plans for the dining hall murals?" Of all the men in Icaria, Fremont was the one Armel had always felt uncomfortable with. Too often, as a small boy, he'd been caught in the swing of Fremont's moods from morose silence to sharp, unfounded anger. But he was curious about the murals, curious enough to risk upsetting the fine balance of Fremont's moods.

Fremont didn't answer, but bent his head to murmur to the cat. Armel took this as consent, and moved around him to the table.

The drawings were on large sheets of the cheap newsprint that the *Revue Icarienne* was printed on. Each sheet represented one panel of a continuous mural whose figures were sketched with charcoal.

"Oh. These are good, Citizen Fremont." Armel felt he should be saying something as he leafed through the stack.

Fremont set the cat loose and lifted the sketches. Carrying them with exaggerated care, he laid them out on the bed, end to end. When he spoke, his voice vibrated with suppressed eagerness.

"You see, it starts here. This is where the door is. This panel shows the creation of the universe, and here the birth of man. Then, as you can see, the progression of civilization, the wars, the suffering, and here in the last panel—Icaria."

Armel tried to imagine these smudged figures blown up to life-size and in color, fighting and bleeding their way around the walls of the dining hall. They'll probably give Gretchen and Louise nightmares, he mused. They may even give *me* nightmares. Aloud he said, "That's really going to be something to see when you get them all done. How long do you think it'll take you?"

"About three months." The eagerness was gone from his voice now. He seemed to resent Armel's eyes on his drawings. He moved between Armel and the sketches, and his face hardened. "What was it you wanted?" he snapped.

Armel withdrew his tentative friendship and rebuilt his own barriers. "It's these boots. You made them way too narrow through the toes. See?" He reached down to pull one off.

"Too narrow! Who are you to tell me the boots are too narrow? You've got wide feet, you hear me? Wide peasant feet. The boots are right. Your feet are wrong! Now get out of my private room with your big stinking feet."

Armel, lining up his arguments, suddenly stopped trying. What was the use of arguing logically with an illogical—madman? And why was it that all of a sudden everyone in the world was out to torment Armel Dupree, to drive him out of his mind with their stupidity? If it wasn't so maddening, it would almost be funny.

"My most humble apologies, oh great one, for my fat feet." Bowing low, he backed out of the cabin. Outside, he stopped to pull off the boots, and oddly, his mood lifted as he loped barefoot across the square toward home.

Cabet was there already, bending over the washbasin on the front stoop. He looked up when Armel tossed his boots into the house, and moved over to make room at the basin.

"Evenin', Cabet. How was everything at the machine shop today? Give me the soap, will you, if you ever get through with it?" It took Cabet forever to get his hands clean before meals, especially around the nails. Armel could wash up in a third of the time.

"Oh, same as usual." It took Cabet forever to answer a simple question sometimes, too. His mind wandered.

"Hey, Cab. Why don't you trade jobs with Jeannie? Then you'd always have clean hands at the end of the day."

Cabet smiled but didn't answer.

"Can't you just see Jeannie wrestling with a ten-foot breaking plow, though?"

A soft snort was Cabet's only reply. The two of them started toward the dining hall. They walked without speaking, Cabet following his own mysterious thoughts and Armel remembering the look on Fremont's face this afternoon, that hating, defensive look.

He must be an awfully unhappy man, Armel thought, although I don't know what he's got to be unhappy about. I wonder how many other people around here are—like Cab, for instance. He's always so darned quiet. I wonder if he's miserable inside about something or other that I don't even know about, or if he's just naturally quiet.

"Cab, what do you want most out of life?" He kept his voice half light.

"To be left alone." Cabet's answer was light, too, implying that it was brothers he wanted to be alone from. But Armel realized Cabet was serious. All their lives Cab had been happiest when people just let him alone. It had been pretty hard on Cab, all those years, being crowded into the cabin. Of course, now he had a whole room to himself. . . .

The dinner horn sounded; immediately there was movement from every corner of the commune toward the dining hall at its hub. The youngsters, Gretchen and Rolfe and Louise and Emil, came cantering. The others came more slowly, from the houses and cabins and from the barns across the road.

Jeannie stood beside the door, holding the horn in one hand and glancing around her, counting the approaching heads, watching for stragglers. She had just lifted the horn to blow again when Armel said, "Shame on you, Jeanne Dupree. Using poor old Grace's horn for a plaything."

She looked at him, startled, then glanced at the cream and gray marbled cow's horn she'd been about to blow.

Armel pressed his advantage. "Poor old Grace, who used to let us ride her all over the pasture and didn't even care when you tied a sunbonnet on her calf that time. Now she's gone to the smokehouse, and you're—"

"Oh, Mel, this was *not* Grace's horn. She had yellowish ones. I remember."

He went on inside. She was always so darned serious about everything, it wasn't much fun teasing her.

Maman and Jeannie had kitchen duty this week,

so he and Cabet and Papa were alone at the Dupree table. They ate in relative silence, as was often the case when Maman and Jeannie weren't there. For lack of anything else with which to occupy his mind while he ate, Armel watched his father and brother from the corners of his eyes. He was struck again with the resemblance between them, despite Papa's beard, Cabet's bad posture, and of course the difference in their ages. Funny that it should have been Cab and Jeannie, the quiet mice of the family, who inherited Papa's tan hair and hazel eyes, while he and Valmor got quiet-mouse Maman's dark coloring. And Papa's contentiousness, he added, smiling down at his plate. He was glad he got what he did, from both of them.

"Boys, we may be moving the printing press into our house." Papa's statement dropped into the silence so abruptly that it took a moment to sink in. When it did, Armel thought, Maybe this is a good time to talk to Papa about my work.

Cabet said, "Are we going to tear down that old cabin, finally?"

Papa nodded. "It should have been one of the first to be torn down. The roof is rotting badly, and there's no way to keep that press from rusting. And the paper is always damp. Besides, having it right there in the house will make my job that much easier."

Armel was just about to speak, when Cabet cut

in. "Where shall we put it? In the little bedroom behind the east front room? You'd have to go through Jeannie's stuff to get back there, but it's the only empty room."

"It will go in my room." It was a definite statement, and it ignored the obvious fact that the room he spoke of was also Maman's.

"But, Papa, that's silly," Armel said. "You'd need four men to carry that heavy thing up those stairs, and somebody could get hurt. Besides, it'd be an awful squeeze, the printing press and all the junk that goes with it, and the big bed and Maman's highboy. When we have a perfectly good *empty* room downstairs, why would you want to . . ."

Papa's eyes wilted the sentence. One simply did not argue with Papa, especially a child. Armel burned with the frustration of having a legitimate argument and not being allowed to exercise it. He changed tactics.

"I've been thinking, Papa; do you suppose there's any chance that I could start helping you edit the *Revue*? I'm a good writer, and I could learn the typesetting part of it in no time. I feel as though I'm. . ." He had started to say "wasted on watching sheep," but that sounded a little conceited. Still, it was true.

Again Papa's eyes were boring through him. At times like this Papa seemed to be looking down on him from a great height, although their eyes were actually on a level.

"And what did you intend that *I* should do after you've taken my job, pray tell? Should I take over your herdsman chores? Or were you planning to retire me at the age of forty-eight?"

Cabet had stopped eating and was looking miserable, as he always did during arguments. Armel was aware that some of the others at nearby tables were listening with amusement. He ignored them.

"Of course not, Papa. But you'll probably be President again next year. It seems as though it's just you and Citizen LeMan anymore, trading off every year, because you two are by far the best Presidents." A little flattery never hurt an argument. "And I didn't mean to take over the *Revue,* at least not for a long time yet."

"It's nonsense." Papa ended the argument.

Anything Papa couldn't justify was nonsense, Armel thought, fighting down the frustration that was knotting his stomach.

"As I started to say," Papa went on, "I'm going to suggest moving the press to our house in Meeting tomorrow night. I wish you boys would both be there."

The next afternoon Armel got his sheep penned up for the night in time to go down to the trestle and

check the melon vines. The four hills had all pro-
duced, even though the sun filtered down to them
between railroad ties. By now, some of the vines
were nearly a foot long. He carried river water to
them in the crock he kept hidden there, and examined
each vine for new growth. Then, aware that it was
getting close to suppertime, he circled around
through the woodlot toward home.

To save time, he decided to clean up at the washhouse rather than at home. He was rolling up his
shirt sleeves beside the well when he heard a shuf-
fling noise above him. The loft over the washhouse
served as a storeroom for the costumes and few stage
sets that were used from time to time for Sunday
entertainments. It was an ideal place to spend an
afternoon if you happened to be a child.

In the loft window above the well Gretchen's
round Germanic face was staring down at him. She
was wearing a huge black hat that had served as
Paris fashion, King Lear, and various other poses.
With Gretchen's apple cheeks and her yellow braids
that hung straight down toward Armel, the hat
merely looked out of place.

"You look like what's-her-name," he called up
to her. "The princess in the tower. Let down your
hair, my lovely one, and I shall climb the tower and
carry you away."

There were titters from the princess and

from Louise in the loft behind her. "I'm not a princess, Mel. I'm Macbeth. Can't you tell? We're going to put on *Macbeth* tomorrow afternoon. Will you come to it?"

"I don't know. If I'm not too busy. But Macbeth was a man."

The face in the window was thoughtful for a moment; then it withdrew. When it appeared again, the yellow braids were stuffed inside the hat. "Now I'm Macbeth. But that's a pretty silly name for a man. Mac*beth*."

Jeannie appeared in the washhouse door. "Oh, Mel. I'm glad you're here. Would you mind taking care of Pepper for me? I have to get on over to the hall and set tables. Thanks."

She was gone around the corner toward the dining hall before he had a chance to agree. The inside of the washhouse was dim and humid, and it smelled strongly of lye soap and of Pepper, the washing machine's horsepower.

"Come on, Peppy. You can stop now." Actually, Pepper looked as though he had never moved and never intended to. He dozed in his harness, one hip sagging, and one back hoof cocked. Armel unhooked the traces from the pole Pepper turned in his endless plodding circle. He tossed the traces across the horse's concave back, then went to the foot of the loft ladder.

"Better come on down now, kids. Almost time to eat." Without having to be led, Pepper followed Armel out of the building and across the road to his barn.

The lanterns in the dining hall flickered as a damp-smelling night breeze crossed the room from open window to open window. It was black and quiet outside the windows, but Armel was sure that Jeannie was listening under the north window. He'd have much preferred to be out there with her and the children, rather than having to sit inside on a hard walnut chair while the meeting dragged along.

The subject that concerned him, whether or not to move the printing press to the Dupree house and tear down the old log cabin that now housed it, had long ago been discussed and voted on. The trouble was, it was considered the height of rudeness to get up and walk out before the meeting was over. They were wrangling now about how much calico, how much linsey-woolsey, and how much Amana blues they should order for the summer sewing. It was bound to be a long argument, because the women could argue but couldn't vote; the only way they could hope to win a point was to argue until the men got sick of hearing them and voted to please their wives.

Armel yawned and shifted on the chair. He'd

always heard that black walnut was one of the hardest woods there was, and now he believed it. He shifted again, but there was no comfort left in the chair after three hours. "This is the last meeting I'm coming to till I'm twenty and *have* to," he muttered to himself.

Suddenly he realized President LeMan wasn't talking about bolts of cloth anymore.

" . . . unfortunate dropping off of our population in recent years, due to the defection of some of our younger members." He seemed to be looking directly at Papa and Maman, across the room from Armel, as though they were responsible for Valmor's leaving.

"Since this is the case, I believe the remaining young members are shirking their duty to Icaria if they continue to remain unmarried, thus depriving Icaria of children to carry on her noble cause."

Silence filled the room. Although there was no sound from the north window, he could feel Jeannie's presence out there, could almost see her leaning toward the window, looking up at the square of light coming out over her head.

"It is my proposition that Cabet Dupree and Berthe Bronner, being the eldest unattached male and female of childbearing age, should immediately set aside whatever selfish hesitancies they may have had . . . "

The voice droned on in its singsong righteousness from the mouth above LeMan's beard. Armel heard no more. He was staring, horrified, across the room to where Cabet sat beside Papa.

Cabet looked at LeMan, stunned.

CHAPTER SEVEN

It was a very quiet Sunday in the Dupree house. Maman said little, but when she passed near Cabet, she touched him, almost absentmindedly as though assuring herself, or him, of something.

Jeannie followed everyone's movements with anxious eyes, watching for signs of a fight, ready to soothe and smooth when the need arose.

Papa made his pronouncement early in the day

and then said no more. "It was voted. It makes sense, and that's the end of it." It occurred to Armel that Papa must have known this was coming. That probably explained why Papa had insisted that the printing press not be put in the east half of the house, the half that was built to house the family of the eldest son.

Armel spent the morning tagging after Cabet, moving to get in front of him when Cab turned away, badgering him with his pointed questions. "Are you going to let them do this to you, Cab? You know you don't want to marry Berthe. Or anyone. You've said that ever since we were grass-high. You wanted to live alone all your life so you'd have time to think about things. Don't you remember all the times you said that? Didn't he, Jeannie?" No answer.

Finally Cabet snapped back. "It was voted on, and it makes sense. Now leave me alone, damn it."

The words were an echo of Papa's, but the strength of Cabet's voice was so unlike Cabet that it startled Armel. He realized then the intensity of what Cab must be feeling behind his quiet face.

Jeannie cleared her throat. "I think it might be fun, having Berthe live with us. I always wanted a sister"—Cabet threw her a look of gratitude—"and she and I can have fun fixing my old room into a sitting room, like it was meant to be in the first place."

The air in the west sitting room had cleared

somewhat a few minutes later when Berthe Bronner looked in at the front door and tapped lightly. Jeannie opened the door for her, giving her a quick, embarrassed hug as she admitted her brother's fiancée.

Armel climbed a few of the stairs that led up to his parents' room, then turned and sat where he could see and hear the whole scene and yet stay outside it. There was a silence over the room, as thick and strained as though Berthe were a mail-order bride and a perfect stranger, rather than someone they all had seen nearly every day of their lives. Armel tried to look at her objectively.

There was nothing outstanding about Berthe Bronner in any way. In a few years she'd probably be too heavy, he thought, eyeing her round face and plump arms. Her hair was curly and usually untidy. She was good-natured and had an easy way with children; Armel remembered being five or six, and Berthe three years older. She'd never been too busy to boost him onto a tree branch or through a high cabin window when he needed help. She'd taught him to swim in the shallow place beyond the mills. Berthe was all right. But not for Cabet. She talked too much, didn't know when to leave a person alone, had never understood Cab's subtle humor. In fact, she'd been an irritant to Cabet as long as Armel could remember.

They were finally talking down there. Cabet was

smiling uncomfortably at Berthe, as though he wanted to let her know she was acceptable to him, for the sake of her pride, and yet not really believing it himself. Maman and Jeannie were carrying the conversation: what Berthe would wear for the wedding, what kind of wild flowers might be in bloom in another month, what furniture Berthe's father would be contributing. . . . Armel quit listening.

By squinting his eyes, he made the figures below seem to grow smaller, farther away. They have the power to do this to him, Armel mused. Even though all Cab ever wanted was to live his life quietly, by himself, they can decide one fine night that he is to be Berthe Bronner's husband, to father as many Icarian babies as Berthe will produce. Armel wasn't rebelling now, just taking a long, wondering look at the power of the Icarian vote.

As he watched Cabet and Berthe, he was aware of an even more frightening aspect. Although Cabet did not want this marriage, was surely hating the idea inside, that full-grown twenty-year-old man down there was placidly allowing them to run his life for him. As a child, Cab had been as spirited, as full of fight, as any boy. Where was that spirit now? Armel felt a chill of fear, not for Cabet, but for himself.

At dinner there was a constrained silence around the Dupree table. The Bronner family sent stiff, bright smiles across the room to Papa and Maman, and were answered in kind.

Where shall I go this afternoon? Armel wondered. Where can I get away from them all? Maybe swimming, if the river isn't too cold. Or maybe rabbit hunting would be better. Yes. I'll get clear out there by myself, maybe get lost in the prairie grass.

The idea was strongly appealing. But when Alexis James caught Armel and Cabet at the door of the dining hall and suggested that the three of them go hunting that afternoon, it no longer seemed such a good idea.

"Come on, Cab, you better come hunting with me. Pretty soon you'll be an old married man, and you'll have to ask Berthe before you can do anything." Alexis' jibes scraped across Armel's nerves.

Cabet shook his head and murmured, "I don't think so today, Lex," and started toward home. But Alexis had never learned to accept the fact that someone might not want his company. He fell into step between Armel and Cabet.

"I was sure glad to hear about you and old Berthe." He jabbed Cabet's ribs with his elbow. "I was afraid they were going to vote her to me. Probably would have, too, if you hadn't been around."

The soul of tact. Armel ground his teeth and kicked at the grass as he walked.

Alexis went on. "Now that you've got Berthe, that leaves me free for Jeannie, hey, brother?"

"Leave him alone, Lex, will you? Just leave him alone!" Funny, Armel thought through his anger, it's supposed to be the big brother who defends the little brother, and here I am fighting Cab's fights again.

With a mumbled excuse to Cabet and Alexis, he turned and headed for the woodlot. As he rounded the corner of the washhouse, he was stopped by a child's voice calling after him. From behind the partly opened washhouse door, Gretchen Hawbaker was peeking out. He could see enough of her to tell she was in some sort of costume.

"Aren't you going to come and watch *Macbeth?* You said you would. The show starts as soon as they get done with the dinner dishes."

He looked down into the solemn little face, searched a moment for a good enough excuse, then gave up and smiled at her. "I wouldn't miss it for the world, Macbeth, your highness. I was just going to get a drink, here. But I'll be in the front row when the curtain goes up."

And why not, he thought. Alexis has spoiled the hunting idea, and the river is probably still too cold for much swimming. Might as well watch the play.

While Gretchen withdrew, giggling, he drew a

bucket from the well and buried his face in the icy water. He blew a couple of soft bubbles through his nose, as he had when he was younger, imitating the horses. Then, wiping his face on his sleeve, he went into the dining hall again and helped to push the round walnut tables back against the side walls and to line up a couple of rows of chairs.

The audience began to assemble. It consisted almost entirely of the Hawbakers and the Coteaus, for Gretchen, Rolfe, and Louise were to be the only actors.

The Hawbaker-Coteau rendition of *Macbeth,* as it unfolded on the low speaker's stand at the end of the dining hall, bore no resemblance that Armel could detect to anything Shakespeare had written. This Macbeth was a girl, because Gretchen had failed in her attempt to keep her braids up under her hat. The acting was lively and almost entirely ad-libbed, and as far as Armel could tell, the story was about two women whose husbands had to go to work.

While his eyes pretended to follow the action on the stage, his mind went back to Cabet and Berthe. He was trying to put himself in Cabet's place, trying to understand what his brother must be feeling about the marriage, when suddenly his mind made a direct and horrifying connection between what he was thinking and what he was seeing.

Cabet was going to marry Berthe Bronner. In

the natural course of events, Jeannie would probably marry Alexis someday—a distasteful thought in itself —and then along would come himself. In a few more years the President was going to stand up on that platform some fine Saturday night and say, "Icaria needs more young married couples producing more Icarian babies, and Armel Dupree is the oldest marriageable bachelor."

And when that time came, the field from which his bride would be chosen was going to consist of just two—Gretchen Hawbaker and Louise Coteau. Those two babies up there in their dress-up clothes, putting on their little-girl play.

Oh, no! His mind tried to reject the idea, but couldn't. It leaped forward, deftly matching up the Icarian children, just as he might choose the right rams for his flock of ewes. He'd have to marry Louise, because Emil Coteau, who was twelve now, could then marry Gretchen. And Rolfe Hawbaker, who was six, could marry Jules Bettanier's little girl, who was just two. Then after that Cabet and Berthe would have children who could marry Alexis' and Jeannie's. . . .

The game his mind was playing fascinated him almost as much as it repulsed him. To marry someone and have to spend the rest of your life cooped up with that person, just because she was the only one your age when marrying time came—no. It was wrong! What if you couldn't stand the person?

He stared hard at Louise Coteau, who now lay across two chairs on the stage, while Gretchen pantomimed a bandaging operation. He'd seen Louise every day of her life, but he'd never actually focused on her. She was as skinny as a snake, with thin black hair and dark eyes that protruded somewhat. Her mouth was too large for her face; her body was all ribs and long sticklike legs and arms. Of course she might get better as she got older, but as a nine-year-old she certainly wasn't very impressive.

Somehow, though, the idea of marrying Louise wasn't as disheartening as it should have been. He simply couldn't take seriously the possibility of its ever happening. It would be at least seven or eight years before she'd be old enough to get married, and *surely* before then something would have happened to change things. Deep down, he couldn't believe that seven years from now he was going to be sitting around here, taking care of sheep, letting the voters assign him to Louise Coteau. The course of things would surely have changed by then. Lord knows, I *hope* so, he thought fervently, as Louise became entangled in the chair back and brought both chairs down upon herself, ending the saga of Macbeth, Icarian housewife.

A light rain was falling outside the dining hall when the play was finished. A good afternoon to read, he thought. Instead of leaving the dining hall with the rest of the audience, he went into the serving pantry at the far end of the room and fixed four thick slices of apricot bread and butter.

The library upstairs was warm, but not uncomfortably so. Setting his bread on a stack of back issues of the *Revue Icarienne,* he opened the one small window, then turned to the shelves of books.

They were the same old books—Papa's law volumes; Citizen Bronner's textbooks, history, economics, and some whose nature Armel wasn't sure of; a couple of shelves of miscellaneous fiction, all of which he'd already read; a few collections of painting reproductions that had been Fremont's. On the top shelf were a handful of novels that had been voted off limits to Icaria's youngsters, but the study bookshelves made an excellent ladder for small climbers. Armel had read all the banned books long ago, along with Alexis and Cabet, and had judged them not worth the bother.

Nothing on the shelves fit his mood this afternoon. He leafed through a few back copies of the *Revue Icarienne,* but found nothing he hadn't already read. Folding his legs gracelessly, he sat on the floor and began a desultory examination of the boxes of old books and magazines that had just been brought up from the cabin which had housed the printing press and was now being torn down.

One of these days I'll have to build some more shelves up here, he mused. This is a mess.

In one box, under a layer of German novels, he found a stack of old issues of what appeared to be a periodical for lawyers. The top issue was dated June, 1846, and it bore the name "Franz Dupree, 21 Rue Royale, Bordeaux" in the upper corner. Armel unfolded the browning paper, wary of its brittleness. The ink was dim, the type crudely set, the columns crooked, but he read the little paper with a growing hunger. Here was a look at the world of lawyers, a world in which Papa had belonged—a world which he himself might be entering right now if Papa hadn't chosen Icaria.

He felt a brief resentment toward Papa, but it was soon lost in the printing before him. He finished the paper and started on the next one. There were articles about unusual cases, personal stories about members of the French legal profession, long editorial dissertations on various aspects of French law.

When he'd finished reading that issue, he pulled the entire stack from its box and moved over to the wall under the window. With his back against the wall, his apricot bread in one hand, and his shoes off, he settled in for a long, engrossing afternoon. He'd read half the stack when he noticed a small article:

"Disbarring proceedings against Franz Dupree, of Bordeaux, were dropped this week, when it was concluded that the defendant had acted in good faith and had committed no actual breach of legal process in his defense of Louis Shagnon in October of last year. Monsieur Dupree has been absolved of responsibility in the unfortunate St. Claire tragedy."

Armel caught his breath. Disbarred? Papa? Impossible. No, of course, it said disbarring proceedings were dropped. But still, the mere fact that Papa had been involved in *anything* that could possibly raise a question of disbarment—it was inconceivable. Armel's mind refused to admit the fact. He read the article again.

Franz Dupree, of Bordeaux. There surely couldn't have been two of them. He looked at the date on the front page. March, 1847.

He began figuring. Let's see, this is 1875. Valmor is twenty-eight this year, and he was born in September. . . . And Papa and Maman left France with the Icarians the spring of that same year, which would have been—seventy-five minus twenty-eight—1847. Just a few months after this was printed. Funny . . .

Suddenly he recalled something he'd heard recently. Who was it—oh yes—the lawyer in Shenandoah who'd given him the pamphlet on Iowa laws.

He had recognized the name Dupree; he had half-remembered hearing about some trouble. But surely this, whatever Papa's trouble was, wouldn't have been common knowledge clear over here in America. But then, whoever Mason had studied law with might have heard about it through some sort of lawyers' grapevine.

But Papa! Papa, who never made a wrong decision or did an unwise thing—getting into any kind of trouble. . . . The thought was provocative and unsettling.

CHAPTER EIGHT

That night the first of Armel's ewes bore twin lambs, and for the next few weeks he had time to think of little beyond keeping track of the newborn lambs, seeing that none was born outside the shelter of the pen. Wolves howled nightly just beyond the farm buildings. For several nights he slept in the loft of the sheep shed, a Kentucky rifle at his fingertips.

Then, when the lambing was done, the shearing

began. An itinerant shearing crew stayed in Icaria for three days, sleeping in two of the unoccupied log cabins and eating at one of the empty tables in the dining hall. The four men spoke little, worked as early and as late as there was sufficient daylight to see by, and departed with their wages from the Icarian treasury, leaving behind mammoth bags of greasy wool and a pasture full of naked sheep.

It was early June now. The corn was six inches tall in the high fields and taller than Armel's boots in the bottomlands. In the vegetable fields west of the commune, the potatoes and sweet corn and beans, the peas and tomatoes and strawberries, were a bright green design on the black loam. The fruit trees in the orchard were bare of their pink and white blossoms, but a close inspection showed small apples, peaches, and cherries, hard and green and abundant. Beyond the Osage orange hedges that separated the fields from the open land, prairie grass waved over the heads of Gretchen and Louise, when they made paths and tunnels through it.

The watermelon vines were growing rapidly, too, although the two hills farthest from the river, and most shaded between the tracks and the bank, were noticeably smaller than the others.

What they need is some fertilizer, Armel thought, as he watched Jules Bettanier carting manure from behind the horse barn to put around the strawberries.

That night, when the long twilight finally turned dark, he sauntered across the road to look in on his sheep. From there, he meandered up past the chicken house and into the horse barn. Swiftly, feeling deliciously like a thief, he filled a gunnysack with forkful after forkful of pungent straw and manure from the pile behind the barn. He circled east along the edge of the high cornfield, across the hedge at the low place where the replacement plants hadn't caught up with the rest of the hedge, then down the steep slope of the sheep pasture to the railroad track below.

The moon was full, the sky so bright with stars that he could clearly see the ties and cinders between the tracks. Locusts chirred; frogs called from the river beyond the cornfield. Somewhere behind him a cow lowed. Beneath these sounds came the constant rush of the river over the mill wheels.

He hoisted the sack a little higher on his back. It pressed across his shoulder. The rough sacking was beginning to chafe his fingers, and the moisture of the load was making itself felt on his back through his shirt. Still, it was a good night to be out, a good night to be young and . . .

A figure stood watching him from the point where the mill road crossed the tracks. In the distorting white moonlight he recognized Alexis James —the last person in the world he wanted to see right now. But Alexis had spotted him already. His mind spinning, searching for a reason why he might be walking down the railroad track at ten o'clock at night with forty pounds of horse manure on his back, Armel approached the waiting figure.

"Armel! What the devil have you—phew. You smell like a walking manure pile. Where you going with that stuff in the middle of the night, anyway?"

A sly smile twisted Armel's mouth. He tried to hide it, but not too hard. When in trouble, look as though you know something no one else does, he told himself. He said nothing, but allowed the smile to speak for itself.

"You're going to play a trick on somebody!" Alexis' voice lowered in conspiracy. "Where are you going to put the manure, Mel? Someplace really good, huh? I'll come with you, all right?"

Armel shook his head firmly. "This has to be done alone, or it won't work. And I can't stand here all night. This stuff is heavy."

He waited until Alexis was halfway up the hill to the commune, and then, knowing Alexis, he left the railroad track and followed the road toward the river. At the corner of the gristmill he set the bag down and, turning his head as little as possible, looked back. As he did so, the small black shadow of Alexis moved off the road, near the crest of the hill, and melted into the dark of the woodlot.

Darned nosy Lex, anyway. Lex the hex. That's what he and Jeannie had named him years ago, when his loudmouthed bumbling spoiled a game of hide-and-go-seek, or scared the fish away from their bait or the prairie hens away from Armel's traps.

When his arms were rested and his fingers unstiffened, he dragged the sack behind the mill, as though he were going to open it there. Then, as fast as his burden allowed, he hoisted the sack and moved through the undergrowth that lined the river. He followed the riverbank at a heavy trot, bending almost double under the sack.

Once he reached the trestle, it took nearly an hour to spread the straw and manure around the melon vines and to work it into the hard-packed earth. His only plow was the jagged half of a pottery crock. When the fertilizer was finally worked in to his satisfaction, he shed his clothes and splashed into the cold green-black river. The swim was a short one, but it washed away the smell, and the blood from the scrapes on his hands, and some of the ache from his muscles. Still, it was a long walk home.

Two days later, on Sunday, the first fishing party of the season was held. The picnic tables were laid at the edge of the river, in the grove of oaks that surrounded the two mills. It was the standard fishing-party meal: French fried potatoes; flapjacks;

fried fish caught early that morning by Citizen Bronner, Jules Bettanier, Peron, and Ponte; rhubarb pie for dessert. All through the meal Armel felt Alexis watching him, sharing the secret, waiting for the fun when the sack of manure showed up in some hilarious place. Armel kept his face blank, his eyes on his plate.

When the meal was over, the men dispersed to the best fishing spots, or walked downstream beyond the sawmill to swim. A few of the women swam too, upriver, weighted down by their water-soaked shifts and bloomers. Jeannie joined the swimmers; Papa and Cabet took their poles and worms and disappeared downriver; Maman and Berthe began scraping and stacking the dishes. While the others went their separate ways, Armel stood around, vaguely watching the children playing a noisy game of Ruth and Jacob around the mill, feeling not exactly like swimming or fishing, but not exactly like doing anything else either. What really appealed to him just then was the long soft grass under a shady tree, a nice nap on a full stomach.

But Alexis was working his way toward him, trying to catch his eye, his face lit with anticipation of Armel's joke. Quickly Armel turned toward Maman.

"Let me help you load those." He lifted the basket of dirty dishes from Maman's arm and set it on the flatbed of the hay wagon that stood in the road. Maman beamed. He felt suddenly guilty that he hadn't thought to help sooner. Alexis hovered by the mill, still trying to catch his eye.

"Hey, Lex. Come on over and help me with these tables, will you?" He smiled brightly and ignored the eager question on Alexis' face. The two of them made short work of dismantling the plank-and-saw-horse tables and loading them onto the wagon with the dishes and chairs and cooking things. Then, when Alexis turned to say something to Berthe, Armel slipped away into the trees, snatched his fishing pole from the grass, and settled down on the bank between Cabet and Citizen Gentry.

It wasn't until late in the evening that Alexis finally cornered him and demanded to know what had happened to the joke about the manure. Armel smiled blankly and shrugged. "Guess it just didn't come off. I thought I had it all rigged." He ducked away, leaving Alexis to ponder. I sure hope those watermelons are worth all the trouble I'm going through for them, he thought, grumbling and smiling.

A few days later Papa made his monthly trip to Corning to mail the *Revues.* The night before, he had finished printing the last of the June issue of the *Revue Icarienne,* and this morning Armel helped him load the twine-tied bundles, two thousand copies in all, into the light wagon. President LeMan handed Papa the pouch with the postage money; Papa accepted it, raised his hand to Maman, and rippled the reins across the horse's back.

Seeing Papa in his town clothes stirred something in Armel's memory. That story about Papa's disbarment—that was it. In the rush of lambing season and then shearing, he'd forgotten it.

"Maman"—he fell into step beside her as she started back toward the bakery—"why did Papa *really* decide to join the Icarians? I mean, I know he agreed with the philosophy and all, but . . ."

She kept walking, but suddenly she was busy fiddling with her apron. Her arms were flour-white to the wrists. Her knuckles and fingernails were permanently etched in white.

"Your papa wanted the best life for his family. This is the best life. The only good life," she recited. "You ask a lot of foolish questions."

"But wasn't there some sort of—trouble—I mean, something about possibly disbarring him? I . . ."

Her bulk swung to face him. "There you do it again with your nonsense. Your papa disbarred? I never heard anything so—"

"The Shagnon case, Maman." He dropped the words quietly into her sputtering. His eyes sought

121

her face. She looked away, but not soon enough to hide the small spasm of recognition. Then she was a stolid blank.

"Your papa was never disbarred. I don't know where you hear such foolishness. Don't you go bothering Papa with such talk."

She strode away from him, then turned and came back more slowly. "Armel, your papa is the wisest man I ever knew. He chose this way of life for us, and it's a good life. We mustn't question." She looked hard at him, her eyes moving back and forth from his left eye to his right. He felt suddenly that he must assure her of something; he didn't know exactly what it was, but he had an idea—and he couldn't give her that assurance.

He didn't bring up the subject of the Shagnon case, whatever it was, but he began to wish there were someone he could talk to about it. Not anyone outside the family, though. Once he almost asked Papa about it, when they were alone on the front step after dinner and Papa was in a better humor than usual. But then he decided it might be wiser not to tamper with Papa's good mood. And somehow, when he looked at Papa's profile in the dark, the whole question of disbarment seemed fantastic. Papa just wasn't the sort of man who got disbarred.

Cabet was of no use as a confidant. He hardly spoke to anyone anymore. He sat through meals with little more than a "pass the bread." He plodded off every morning to the machine shop, then plodded home again and read in his room after supper as long as the daylight lasted. It seemed to Armel that Cab was cramming his days as full of solitude as he possibly could, storing up enough to last through the coming years of marriage.

That left only Jeannie, and Armel couldn't quite bring himself to tell her about the Shagnon trial. She was so positive Papa could do no wrong that Armel couldn't allow himself to crack her beautiful unquestioning belief.

He did try to get her started talking about how she felt about Icaria one evening. It was the night before Cabet's wedding. The rest of the family, including Cabet, were at Meeting. Jeannie had stayed home to put some finishing touches on the east parlor, the room that had been her bedroom and would now be the parlor of Cabet and Berthe. Armel helped her shift the furniture that had been moved from next door. Then, when the room was arranged the way she thought Berthe wanted it, the two of them went out and sat on the front step.

The insects were loud, the voices from the dining hall muffled. They followed their own thoughts for several minutes before Armel said, "I wonder what Cab's thinking about right now."

Jeannie shrugged. "About Berthe, I suppose."

From the woodlot behind the house came the sudden loud rasping of locusts.

"Jeannie?" Silence. "Did it ever occur to you that Papa might have had some—well, some reason for joining the Icarians—I mean some reason we don't know about?"

She snorted, but didn't dignify the suggestion with an answer.

His mind wandered off. It probed a while around the Shagnon case, then meandered to the pamphlet on Iowa laws. He'd been reading it again from time to time for no special reason.

I wonder what you have to do to get disbarred in Iowa, he mused. If you were a lawyer here . . . The picture of the law office in Shenandoah appeared, then faded. Darn, if I could just . . .

His voice sounded far away when he said, "What's the one thing you want most in the whole world?" Jeannie didn't answer. "You must want something. Everybody wants something."

Still she didn't answer, but he could feel her thinking about the question. When he'd given up on her answering, she spoke in a voice so low he could barely hear. "You asked, so I'll tell you. But, Mel, if you laugh at me, I'll hate you." She paused, forming her words. "The one thing I want, and I know it's wrong, and I don't *really*—but sometimes I wish I could have just one man to take care of. I'd like to do everything for my one man, cook his meals and, well, take care of him. Wash his clothes and only his, instead of doing the laundry for every man in Icaria. When I have a husband, I'm going to love him so much that I'll want to take care of him all by myself, and not have Citizenne LeMan cooking his meals and Maman baking his bread and Citizenne Bettanier sewing buttons on his shirts."

She cut herself off and dropped her eyes to the ground. For a long time neither spoke. This was a side of his sister he'd never suspected—and an aspect of the Icarian way of life he'd never considered. Quietly he said, "I wonder if Berthe feels the same way?"

CHAPTER NINE

The wedding took place the next morning, Sunday, at ten o'clock in the dining hall. Cabet, in Papa's town suit, and Berthe, in peach-colored velvet, stood holding hands in front of the speaker's platform while President LeMan read the brief Icarian marriage service. Armel sat between Papa and Jeannie in the loose rows of chairs.

The ceremony was exactly like the only other

one he'd seen, Jules and Marie Bettanier's, three years ago. In fact, the dress Berthe was wearing was the same one Marie had worn. On Berthe it was much too tight, and since the Bettaniers' wedding the white lace on the front had yellowed noticeably. Somewhat to his surprise, Armel found himself pitying poor dense Berthe. But then, thinking of Berthe's incessant pointless talking, he transferred his sympathy to Cabet.

LeMan's voice ceased. He smiled as he closed the folder containing the Icarian bylaws and services. There was an awkward instant when Cabet dropped Berthe's hand, didn't realize he was supposed to kiss her upturned waiting face, finally did realize it, and bent toward her at the same time that she lowered her reddened face. His kiss hit somewhere near her eyebrow. As he watched, Armel felt his own face go red in sympathy with Cab, and the bride.

Chairs scraped back as everyone rose and converged on the narrow center aisle. Citizen Bronner and his wife, Maman and Papa, exchanged handgrips, teary smiles, quick hugs between the mothers. Armel stood back and watched the scene. Then, as the bride and groom joined their parents and the cluster of men and women who were gathering in the center of the room, he rushed forward and gave Berthe a quick, stiff half-hug. He grasped Cabet's hand, gripped his brother's arm tightly with his other hand, and could find nothing to say.

He heard Maman laughing gently behind him. When he turned, Maman had one arm around Jeannie's shoulder. Jeannie's face was blotched and stretched with crying and trying to smile.

". . . being silly, Chérie. You cry at funerals, not at weddings." Maman's voice was bubbling, chiding, happy.

Sniffling and smiling, Jeannie moved forward to hug her new sister-in-law and Cabet. As her eyes moved past Armel's face, he had the uncomfortable sensation that Jeannie's tears were not entirely due to the happiness of the occasion.

Dinner was early and more festive than usual. This was Citizenne Bronner's week for cooking duty, and she had outdone herself. So had Maman in the bakery. The wedding cake that followed the meal was huge and ornate and delicious.

For an hour or so after dinner there was little activity in any of the houses around the commune. Then, as the effects of overeating began to wear off, the usual Sunday afternoon pastimes were taken up. For Armel it seemed a letdown. The wedding was over, and everything was back to normal already.

Almost normal, anyway. In the Dupree house, there was a change. Armel no longer had a room to go to when he needed to be alone. His room behind the parlor was now Jeannie's. She was a girl and needed her own room more than he did. At least that was Maman's theory. The logic escaped Armel. His bed was now in the corner of the parlor, next to the stairway. Cabet had built a row of pegs in the wall for his clothes and a small storage chest, low enough to slide under the bed, for his personal belongings. But there were no doors he could close.

"After seventeen years cooped up in that old cabin," he told himself, "it sure didn't take you long to get spoiled about having a room to yourself."

The door at the foot of the stairs that separated the east and the west parlors would stay closed most of the time now, since it separated the homes of the Franz Dupree family and the Cabet Dupree family. Armel wandered from the parlor-bedroom to his old room, where Jeannie was arranging her things, to the upstairs bedroom, where Maman lay asleep across the big bed. The room was stifling. The printing press and its paraphernalia took up all the space between the bed and the highboy, making the room seem even hotter.

Maman lay on her back, her beefy arms flung wide, her hair pulled loose from its knot. Her mouth was open slightly, and it seemed to Armel that she looked sadder, sleeping, than she ever did awake. He left her and went down to the river for a swim.

The part of the river that was designated for

men's swimming was wider and deeper than the rest of the shallow river, but it had the disadvantage of a mud bank. This stretch of river was deserted this afternoon, but Armel could hear voices from upstream, where the women swam. Better leave my drawers on then, he decided. He skinned out of the rest of his clothes and did a shallow dive from the grassy bank out over the mud and into the green-brown water. When he came up, Citizen Bronner was watching from the bank.

"Come on in and get cooled off," Armel called. "The water's not very cold, but it's better than standing out there." He was glad for the company.

Bronner sucked his pipe reflectively, then began to get ready for his swim. He stripped to his union suit, made sure his pipe was going to stay lit, and, with a practiced motion, parted his beard and tied the two ends in a loose knot behind his head. With professorial dignity he walked downstream to where the mud disappeared, and waded into the water. He didn't actually swim, but he did lower his stout gray-clad form below water level and move his arms along the water's surface until he was close to Armel.

For a while Armel swam around him, trying not to make waves big enough to douse the pipe. Then he came back and let his feet touch bottom beside Bronner. His arms floated out on the surface of the chest-deep water. Bronner's head gleamed pink in the sun that came in narrow shafts through the trees. The shouts and splashing that came to them from the women's part of the river accented the quiet here.

"It was a nice wedding," Armel said.

"Yes indeed."

"Citizen Bronner, would you tell me something, honestly? What do you really think about the wedding? I mean, not just Cab and Berthe, but—the fact that, well, I don't think Cab really wanted to get married. Nothing against Berthe," he added quickly.

Bronner puffed on his pipe, squinted into the sun, puffed and squinted until Armel was afraid he'd forgotten the question.

"Pup, when you get older, you'll understand the wisdom of a marriage like this."

Armel waited, but that was all the explanation there was. "But do you think it's *right*?"

Bronner opened his eyes and sent a benign smile across the sun-dappled water that came to his chin. "You're seventeen, son. At your age it's only right that you should have some questions. All I can say to you is that the rest of us are older and a little wiser, and you must just have faith in us. Eventually you'll understand. You young ones are the bright hope of Icaria—Cabet and Berthe and Jules and the others, but especially Armel Dupree." He removed his pipe and pointed the stem at Armel.

"I have great faith in you, pup. You're going to be a leader, and in the years to come Icaria must have a leader like you, or it won't survive. Icaria will always have enemies on the outside, Mel, but her biggest danger lies right here, in the hidden demon of greed inside all of us."

Armel flung himself back onto the water and, shutting his eyes against the sun, floated away from Bronner. He didn't want vague talk about the demons of greed, and he didn't want to hear how much Bronner and Icaria were counting on him. What he wanted was answers. He turned over and began to swim upstream until some of his frustration eased out through the hard pull of his arms and the furious kicking of his legs. When he came back downstream, Bronner stood quietly talking to himself in the middle of the river.

Ordinarily the Fourth of July was the one day of the year when all of Icaria went to town. This year Fremont stayed behind to work on his murals.

Everyone else left as soon as breakfast and the necessary morning chores were out of the way. The two hay wagons and the horses that pulled them were strung with red, white, and blue bunting. A few of the older members, Catherine Noir and Alexis' grandfather, rode on chairs lashed to the floor of the front wagon. On that wagon, too, were the middle-aged, those young enough to sit on the hard boards of the wagon bed, but too old to join the noisier second wagon.

Jules Bettanier drove the second wagon. Its riders were Cabet and Berthe; Marie Bettanier and the baby; Armel; Jeannie; Alexis; Peron and Ponte, who were nearly forty but seemed younger, probably because they weren't married; and the children, Gretchen and Rolfe, Louise and Emil. The songs they sang were mostly in English. They drowned out the softer French songs that floated back to them from the old folks' wagon.

The four miles to Corning were long ones. The sun was merciless, the road thick with dust that rose from the front wagon to choke the riders behind. It was a straight road, heading due west through unkempt open prairie and fields of corn, but it dipped and rose sharply in several places, so that the horses were alternately lying forward into their harnesses or bracing themselves against the downhill push of their wagons. In the uncultivated stretches the prairie grass waved higher than the horses' heads, so that, when the road curved, the front wagon was lost from sight for a few minutes, to the delight of Gretchen and Louise.

By the time they got to the ford at the edge of Corning, Armel's good Amana blues were wet with sweat. His voice was hoarse from singing; his stomach ached and rumbled in anticipation of the picnic.

The ford was one of the best in southern Iowa, with its broad shale base and gradually sloping banks. The wagons crossed the river without so much as a wet bunting. By now the road was clogged with wagons and riders on horseback. The half mile from the ford to the courthouse square took nearly half as long as the entire four-mile ride from Icaria. The road widened as it wound northwest through the trees and buildings of Corning. There were two blocks of store buildings set on a wide north and south street. At the far north end, the street split and encompassed the small wooded courthouse square. The square lay on a hillside, so that the courthouse rose above the rest of the town.

The Icarians tied their teams under the trees in the far corner of the square and spread their picnic quilts as close together as possible. The thought crossed Armel's mind that it might have been nice to eat among strangers just once. But he forgot it as the food emerged from the hampers.

After lunch, while almost everyone else moved their blankets and chairs toward the bandstand in the center of the square in preparation for the speeches, Armel wandered down the slope of the park and out into the unshaded glare of the street. Speeches he could do without. They'd be long and so uniformly fervent that their fervency would lose its power. The speakers would be unknown to him, unrelated to his life in any way, just as the things they'd shout about were unrelated to Armel Dupree. He knew this from a lifetime of Independence Day celebrations. It was the chance for a day in town that was important, not the speeches.

He scuffed down the sidewalk, hands in pockets, bouncing slightly with the spring of the boards beneath his feet. The broad dusty street beside him was empty except for a knot of youngsters on horseback at the corner a block away. He passed a saloon, the bank, an empty lot. In front of the harness shop he paused and stared in at the hames and bridles and double-stitched traces. He went on, passing another empty lot—not so many empty lots, though, this year as there were last Fourth.

From behind him the hot breeze carried snatches of what the first speaker was saying. ". . . more precious than that freedom for which . . . gave their lives so that you and I . . ."

He stopped to squint through the glass front of the newspaper office. Freedom. Freedom. The word drifted about in his mind until it caught his attention, and then he was intrigued not by the importance of the word but by its utter lack of meaning.

What freedom? What is it, anyway? Do I have

it? I must. I'm an American. Or am I an Icarian and therefore *not* an American? No, that's silly.

All right then. What is my freedom? I am free to—let's see—be what I want? No. . . . Go where I please, live where I want? Well, I could. I'm not a prisoner or anything. But I couldn't just pick up and move to another town. Not without changing everything in my life. So then. Free to—make something better of myself than what I am now? Sure. Sure? Well, I could work harder at the sheep business. If I wanted to. Yes, but why should I? What difference would it make?

He began to feel uncomfortable. Too much lunch, probably.

All right then, he argued silently, say maybe I don't have this so-called freedom. How about them, all those other people that have it? Are they happier than I am, really?

He was sweating profusely now; the sun glared on the tin roof of the hotel across the street, blinding him. Into his head came crowding all the things he'd heard all his life, all the reasons, the good, logical reasons, why the communistic life of Icaria was so far superior to the way other people lived. Freedom was nothing; security, brotherhood, the perfect fairness of the Icarian way, that was the good of life. Possessions bred inequality and greed. . . .

His head ached. Besides, it was a holiday. No

time for thinking deep thoughts. He was at the intersection now, where a smaller street crossed the main street, dividing the business section into two blocks. This lower block held mostly saloons and ended at the railroad depot. Armel could see the sun glinting off the tracks, the same tracks that sheltered his watermelons. He smiled. Thinking of his melons, he realized that if possessions were evil, then he must be evil, because he possessed at least a dozen half-grown, pale green watermelons. The smile lit his face.

In the shade of the Farmers' Mercantile on the corner, he stopped to watch the riders whose horses were milling in the intersection. Most of them were boys younger than he. There were a few girls, riding astride in split dresses. They were too young, he knew, to be allowed to compete in the races later in the day. So they were having their own races now. He watched with half-attention while they lined up, sometimes in pairs, sometimes seven or eight abreast, and thundered down the street to the depot, turned and thundered back.

As he watched, Armel decided that probably several of those young riders owned the horses they rode. Maybe owned the saddles and bridles. He tried to imagine himself in their place. Armel Dupree, mounted on a leggy bay three-year-old that he had raised from a colt, trained himself, took care of himself, allowed no one else to ride . . .

He shook his head sharply, smiled a rueful smile at himself, and wandered on down the street.

It wasn't until hours later, on the ride home after the speeches and races and picnic supper and fireworks, that he found himself thinking about that handful of shouting, shoving, galloping children—and thinking about that word *freedom* again. He sat hunched on the tail of the wagon, staring at the road unwinding itself below his dangling feet. In his preoccupation he didn't even hear Jeannie and the others singing behind his back.

Those boys back there in town, riding their horses or their fathers' horses, *they* had freedom. If one of them wanted to be a lawyer or a storekeeper or whatever, chances are he could go ahead and at least try to be it. If he didn't succeed, it would probably be because he didn't have what it took. Not because some power-hungry old man with a beard down to his belly button said, "Sorry, we don't need what you want to be. You'll have to be a manure shoveler."

That's not quite fair to President LeMan, he thought, grinning. He's not really power-hungry. But he does have a beard clear down—

"Mel, you aren't singing. Come on. Girls start out "Frère Jacques"; boys take the second part." Jeannie nudged him with her toe.

When Armel turned, he saw that Alexis had wedged himself in close beside Jeannie. He saw the sparkle and flush of her face, and the way she was letting her hair blow. The discontent he'd kept buried all afternoon rose to sharp melancholy. He was different from the rest of them, separate from them, and on this blue-black summer night he hated his separateness.

In spite of his exhaustion Armel woke earlier than usual the next morning. He padded to the window and squinted out at the sun. I'll just about have time to go take a look at the melons before everybody else is up, he decided.

It was becoming harder all the time to get down to the trestle and back without arousing curiosity. A couple of times he'd run into Alexis, and it seemed to him that Lex was unusually interested in where he had been.

He pulled on his pants and went out onto the dew-soaked grass, bare chested and barefoot. The sun was just clearing the roofs of the barns. Shadows of trees and buildings were long and blue in cool contrast to the yellow-green of the grass. He looked around, turning slowly full circle, partly to see if anyone was up and out yet, partly in pleasure at having such a nice world all to himself.

At this moment he loved this place—the buildings tinted pink by the sunrise; the poplars behind Catherine's cabin; the men and women asleep in every house he could see, who were an extension of his family, knowing him, taking care of him. He closed his eyes and raised his arms in an aching stretch, and it seemed to him that if he leaned back, all of Icaria would reach out to keep him from falling. If there was a price to pay for the security Icaria gave him, he couldn't feel it this morning.

In the woodlot he passed a pair of sows lying flat on their sides under a pine. Each had a row of pigs down her belly, dozing and sucking and twitching. The sows lifted their heads to peer out from beneath flapping ears as he walked by.

"Good morning, ladies. Don't let me disturb you."

Halfway down the slope he nearly stepped into a miniature rock garden. At least that's what it appeared to be. It was an oval, maybe two by three feet, outlined with small stones from the river. There were no caterpillars inside this time, only flowers. He squatted for a closer look.

The little garden showed the fine hand of Gretchen and Louise, all right. There were at least a couple of almost every kind of wild flower around —prairie clover, primroses, deep blue downy gentian, snow trillium, white lamb's tongue, a few he couldn't name. The girls had evidently picked the flowers, then planted the severed stems in the ground; some of them were beginning to wither already. He touched a leaning gentian stem, and the flower toppled.

He smiled to himself as he rose. To think one of those flea-brained girls was probably going to be his wife some horrible day. But for an instant, as he walked away, he was glad they'd built their silly garden where he'd seen it.

The melons looked good. They were about half grown now, twelve of them as nearly as he could count, hard and pale and promising. That would make twelve muggy summer evenings when the Duprees could sit on the front step and divide a cold, sweet, wet, meaty melon among them. His stomach rumbled, thinking about it.

Of course, he thought, Maman will probably want to share them with the Bronners and Catherine and one or two of the others. Maybe I'll just give Maman the first one and tell her about the others, and then she can do what she wants with them. She can give one to everybody. If she wants. But they'll be *my* gift to her. And Papa, of course. To her and Papa. It may be the only time in my life I have anything that's mine to give away. I wonder if they'll understand how important that is to me. Or if they'll think I was really breaking the rules.

As he started back toward breakfast, he was

aware that his mood had changed slightly, had darkened a little in the last few minutes from the shadow of a thought that hadn't quite materialized. But it was too nice a morning for dark moods. The sun hit him full in the face, warming him. He decided to think about how he should make the Big Melon Presentation. Would it be better to try to sneak one into the house or. . . Gradually the depression faded.

He had just left the railroad tracks for the wood-lot when he heard a shrill, angry cry.

"Darn you, darn you, darn you! I hate you! Get away, you stupid old . . ."

At the spot where the rock garden had been, Louise Coteau stood, beating with fury on the back of one of the sows. The little girl wore only her nightgown; her hair was spiky and uncombed; her face wet with angry tears. The sow, impervious to the pounding fists on her back, was slowly and thoroughly rooting out the garden's flowers and eating them.

Armel drove the sow a few yards away, but the garden was scattered and churned and torn beyond repair.

Louise turned on him. "Your stupid pigs! That's the third garden they ate! Armel, can't you build a pen for them? Can't you keep them shut up? Those stupid, stupid pigs! I wanted to come out and visit my beautiful garden before anybody else got up, and there she was, *eating* it!" Louise aimed an impotent kick in the sow's direction.

She was making such a big issue of it that suddenly the whole thing seemed rather silly. The flowers would have been dead by afternoon anyway.

"Now, Louise, you know very well if the pigs were penned up, they wouldn't get enough to eat. They have to have the run of the woodlot. Besides, Bronner's in charge of them. I'm the sheepman, remember? The pigs aren't my . . ."

The sentence hung in the air. Louise turned away and dropped to her hands and knees to retrieve the rocks. He left her and started to climb the slope through the trees toward the commune. "Better come on and get dressed, Louise. Breakfast, pretty soon." His words were automatic and barely loud enough to carry back to her.

The pigs aren't my responsibility, he thought. Like the chickens weren't Alexis' responsibility that day when they were out in the rain. Like the cows, when they got into the green corn and Alexis and Peron and Ponte just stood around and watched. Am I getting to be that way, too?

He felt, in his stomach, a clench of fear.

CHAPTER TEN

The potato field was muggy-warm, even though there was an hour yet until sunrise. In the shadowy light from what was left of the moon, Armel searched the leaves of the potato plant, found his black and yellow striped target, and mashed it with deft fingers. The ground was moist under his knees; the potato leaves were soaked with dew. Invisible cold strands of spider webs laced his arms and face.

He rocked back on his heels and looked across the rows at his fellow workers—Gretchen and Louise, Emil and Rolfe. And their little helper, Armel Dupree, the field hand, the seventeen-year-old potato-bug picker. Self-disgust, and an odd sense of unreality, shivered through him. What am I doing here? I've taken a wrong turn somewhere along my life. I shouldn't be here. I should be . . .

He searched for the right words. His instincts told him he should be somewhere else, doing something else. Making a start toward a goal. Not picking potato bugs, not counting noses in the sheep pen.

"Going to be a hot one today," he said aloud. Emil Coteau, in the next row, turned and looked and grunted. Armel flipped a mashed bug at Emil, but the boy had already gone back to work.

Armel snorted. The younger generation sure is a bunch of sobersides. I wasn't like that when I was twelve.

He shrugged off his fellow pickers and turned his mind to more interesting thoughts. Tomorrow. The big day. "W" day. I'll make the presentation after supper, when Maman and the rest of them are sitting around on the front step. It'll still be plenty hot enough for that ice cold watermelon to . . .

His eyes unfocused as he thought about that first cold bite dissolving against the roof of his mouth. He could just see the looks on all of their faces when he came around the corner of the house with that big melon in his arms, dripping river water.

I'll have to be sure to get down there sometime today and pick out the best one and put it in the river, so it can have plenty of time to chill.

"Hey, Mel. Did you go to sleep? We're getting way ahead of you." It was Louise's brown face leering at him across the rows. The others *were* getting ahead of him. He moved to the next plant, all business now.

He had finished his row and was helping Gretchen catch up, when the first rays of the sun lit the field. When it did, the remaining potato bugs stirred, spread their beetle wings, and rose into the air.

Armel sighed. "Okay, I guess that's it for this morning." They stood, stretched, and plodded back down the rows toward the commune.

Emil, at the front of the procession, turned and called, "It's going to rain today. I can hear it in the poplars."

A double row of Lombardy poplars separated the vegetable gardens from the commune. As he neared the trees, Armel listened to the whispered rustle they made. Emil's right, he thought. It does sound like rain.

The thundershowers rolled in during the middle of the afternoon. Armel was in the woodlot, on his way back from the trestle, where he had half-buried the choice melon in the sand of the riverbank, beneath the water. He could hear the rain on the leaves above and around him as he climbed the woodlot slope, but only a few stray drops touched him. He looked up through the green roof and reveled in his immunity.

Coming out of the woods behind the little stone bakery, he could see Maman through the window. She'd be making the supper bread now, or maybe something for dessert. Her back was toward the window, her head bowed, as though she were reading from her recipe notebook. The fire from the baking ovens lit the room and outlined Maman's square, weary shape. He thought of how proud she was going to be when she found out that he'd grown all those watermelons and kept them a secret, just so he could surprise her.

I think I'll surprise her right now, he decided. I'll sneak up under the window and wail like a ghost. No, I'll do my eagle call.

But when he got to the window and looked in again, he could see that what she was reading was not recipes. It was a letter. Looking over her shoulder, he could see the large folded sheet, the blue ink scrawls. It was a personal letter. But who would write Maman, that she wouldn't show the letters to the rest of the family? Oh, of course. He answered himself. Valmor! Maman had a letter from Valmor! But still, why wouldn't she show it to the rest of them?

The rain chilled his neck and molded the shirt to his back. Hunching his shoulders against the clammy chill of it, he moved closer to the window. Maman wasn't reading the letter, just looking down at it as though she'd already memorized it and just wanted to hold it, to look at it. She turned, folded the letter with automatic motions, and reached to slip it under a stack of muffin pans on the top shelf. Before she could turn again toward the window, Armel was gone.

At the supper table he was preoccupied. Jeannie had to nudge him twice to get him to pass things. He wondered if he should come right out and ask Maman about the letter. No, she'd just shut herself off, and probably bawl him out for peeking in the window at her. But the letter couldn't go uninvestigated. Tonight, he thought, I'll go read it while everybody's at Meeting.

With that decision made, he brought his mind back to the dining room. There were only four at their table now. Cabet and Berthe had their own table across the room. He stared from the corners of his eyes at his sister-in-law and wondered if Cab was right in what he'd told Armel last night. Berthe pregnant already. They were going to announce it at Meeting tonight, and wouldn't all the old beards be glad. Another generation for Icaria. Another name for the increasingly short roll call. This would make them happier than a new purebred Percheron foal.

He felt slightly cynical, slightly amused. And again, slightly separated from the rest of them.

He'd intended to go to Meeting himself tonight to raise the question of a better job. Through the summer months his feeling of frustration, of going to waste, of needing to try himself at something he wasn't sure he could do, had grown to the point where it seldom left him completely. Papa's job of editing, writing, and printing the *Revue Icarienne*, to be sent to France and to other communes in America, was really about the best job in Icaria, for him anyway. It took the most intelligence. Not everyone had the ability to do it—and Armel felt a strong, deep assurance that he could do it, and do it better than Papa, given a few years.

But of course, the newspaper was Papa's job.

And Icaria didn't need a lawyer. A wry grin twisted his face. No, the perfect society had no crime. And if it did, there was the President and the voters to dole out justice. So no one would ever know that Armel Dupree was potentially a good lawyer. An outstanding lawyer, as good as Papa.

He sighed. No one will ever know that. I'll never know—for sure.

But I won't go to Meeting tonight and listen to

them crowing over Berthe, watching poor dumb Cabet, who still doesn't know he was railroaded. I won't beg them for a better job and give them the satisfaction of their righteous arguments. I'll sneak around to the bakery and see what's in that letter.

It was nearly eight o'clock when the meeting finally got under way, but there was still enough daylight for Armel to find the letter under the muffin tin. He took it to the window and tipped it to catch the light.

It *was* from Valmor, and, Armel realized as he read, it was not the first letter Maman had received from him. Did Papa know about them, he wondered. Was she keeping them a secret from the whole family, or just from him? He felt angry, as he had when he was small and adults spelled mysterious words to each other over his head.

The letter's first paragraph described a room Valmor had recently rented, comparing it with "the last place." He went on to say that things were going well for him "at the office."

Armel looked at the top of the page and saw the return address. Des Moines. All these years since Val left, he thought, all this time I've been wondering and wondering where he was, and what he was doing, and I hardly dared to mention his name in the house. And here Maman has been getting letters from him all along. She knew how much it would have meant to me to know how he was doing. He's my brother. She had no right not to tell me.

He turned the letter over and read on. "Has Armel changed his mind yet about coming up here? Even though I haven't seen him for years, it's hard to believe that the Armel I remember is still content in Icaria. Ask him again, Maman, please. I have an extra bed here. And I know so many people in Des Moines by now that I'm sure I could help him get started at a career. Does he still read Papa's law books? The need for lawyers is great. It would be easy to find someone willing to teach a bright youngster like Mel."

The remainder of the letter blurred before his eyes as he realized the full meaning of what he had read. A chance had been offered him, a chance to test himself in a non-Icarian world and to compare that world with this one. Maybe he wouldn't have accepted Val's offer. Maybe he'd have accepted it and found that Maman and Papa were right. But she hadn't even intended to let him know the offer had been made!

He returned the letter to its hiding place and went out into the fast-falling darkness. His first anger at Maman receded before the overwhelming possibility of what Valmor had suggested. The door had been opened for him. If he wanted to leave

Icaria, he could just pack up and go. His brother would give him a place to stay, would help him understand the non-Icarian existence. Val would show him how to start studying law in earnest. It could all be done.

And all it would cost was what it would do to Papa and Maman. If two sons deserted Icaria, what would it do to them?

He kicked at a tuft of grass. It was dark enough now for the fireflies to be out. At the front steps of his home he turned and sat down. His eyes followed the dipping blinking fireflies, but his mind was unaware of them.

His thoughts circled as fruitlessly as a dog in pursuit of his tail. Maman had no right to decide that I shouldn't even know about Valmor's offer. But do I have the right to put her through all that misery and humiliation again? She took it so hard when Val left. But then, what I really have to decide is, what is the best thing to do with my life, because I'm the one who'll have to *live* the decision, not Maman or Papa or anyone else.

He looked around the commune, from the black squares of the houses and cabins—there was a light in Catherine's window, he noticed—to the dining hall, where lights and voices came out the open windows.

The realization was seeping through him that

he actually did have a choice to make. No longer was it a question of "someday years from now." If he was going, now was the time, and here was the opportunity. He strained to imagine himself in that world of Val's—renting rooms and buying food and clothes with money someone paid him for his labor or services; owning a horse, a pair of boots, a gun that could not be taken away from him and reassigned to someone else, things which by their superior quality would reflect the quality of their owner. He thought about having to depend solely on his own intelligence and integrity with no commune behind and around him, sometimes irritating him but always seeing that his needs were met.

What kind of man would I turn out to be? he asked himself with as much honesty as he possessed. Would I be able to keep on making myself work, even after the fun wore off? Would I find out I'm not as smart as I think I am, when I have to compete with other men?

He knew then that the choice that faced him went deeper than a choice between farming or being a lawyer, deeper than living in Icaria or in another town. The choice was, simply, whether the Icarian way was right or wrong, or at least whether it was right or wrong for Armel Dupree. As the question became clearly defined, brought into focus to be examined, a small uneasy shadow that had followed him all summer lifted and disappeared. He smiled.

Lying in bed that night, after everyone was home and the house settled down, Armel remembered that tomorrow was Watermelon Day. At first he laughed at himself for making such a big thing of a few watermelons. But then, thinking about how few nice things he'd ever done for anyone in his family, and how he might possibly be hurting Maman very much when he'd reached his decision, he was glad that there was something he could give her now.

The next evening after supper he instructed Maman and Papa, Jeannie, Cab and Berthe, to sit on the front steps and wait for a surprise. They looked properly mystified, but they sat, although Papa sighed his impatience. Armel loped down the woodlot hill, laughing at himself for enjoying this so much.

The melon was waiting. He plunged his arms into the cold river and brought up the melon, chilled, dripping, heavy and slick in his arms. He turned. Alexis stood watching.

"Ah, good. It's ripe. I thought they'd never get ripe, Mel. Don't you think you ought to bring a couple more, though? One melon isn't going to go very far, divided among the whole commune, is it?"

154

CHAPTER ELEVEN

His arms and the melon grew dry in the hot evening
breeze as Armel stared from Alexis to President
LeMan. For a long time no one spoke.

Finally President LeMan broke the silence.
"Alexis told me one of our members was hoarding,
but I would never have suspected you, Armel."

Armel had been braced for anger, not sadness.
He didn't know what to say. He cleared his throat.

155

"The seeds were given to me, sir. I didn't think of it as hoarding. I did all the work. I was just going to give them—to the family. . . ."

LeMan stood on the ridge of the riverbank above Armel's head. In his black Sunday suit, with a mass of sunset-tinted clouds behind him and his waist-long beard parted and tossed by the wind, he was awesome.

"You hid these melons from the others deliberately in order to keep them for yourself. You have violated the most basic and vital of our laws, Armel. I can't impress on you strongly enough what a dangerous thing this is, that you've done to us."

The doubt Armel had tried to bury all summer burst into view. So, they were going to regard it as a crime. In spite of his fury, he couldn't help scoffing at that.

LeMan went on talking over Armel's head while the melon grew unbearably heavy. The President's words floated out over the riverbed like maple wings, some blowing away, a few settling in Armel's mind. ". . . threat to the very foundation of Icaria . . . sure you *meant* no real harm . . . a selfish child's thoughtless act . . . must not be allowed to pass unpunished."

As LeMan talked and Alexis smirked, an odd feeling of straightness and strength began to grow in Armel. He set the melon down and stood with his feet planted firm in the sand. For once his hands hung quietly at his sides without needing to tuck themselves into pockets or belts for support. He had, for the first time in his life, a strong, heady feeling of belonging to himself.

He strode up the bank to stand in front of LeMan. Their eyes were on a level.

"Now, Armel. I don't want to be any harder on you than necessary. I want to be fair. We'll vote . . ."

But Armel was already walking away, his back stiff with disdain.

The mood held until he was almost home, then melted into fury and frustration. The whole family was waiting for their surprise on the porch steps where he'd left them. Their expressions of anticipation dissolved when they saw him.

"Mel, what's the matter?"

"Where's the surprise?"

He stood before them and looked at every face except his father's. "The surprise has been impounded, that's what's the matter. I'm going to kill Alexis James one of these days, that little wart." He told them about the watermelons, dramatizing, in his anger, LeMan's accusations and Alexis' vindictiveness.

Jeannie was the first to react. "Oh, Melly, you worked so hard just so you could surprise us. That's the nicest thing anyone's ever done. Sit down here. I'm going to go get you some cider."

"Watermelons," Berthe mused. "I haven't had watermelons but once in my life."

"Well, you're not going to get them now," Armel snapped. He sank down to where Jeannie had been sitting, and stared off across the square to where Fremont was coming out of his cabin to begin his nightly painting in the dining hall.

It'll be all over Icaria before morning, he thought. I wonder who's going to be on my side. If any.

Maman said, "That was a very nice thought, you wanting to give us the melons. But you know President LeMan is right. It was hoarding. What are they going to do about it?"

"Take a vote next Saturday." Armel's voice was low and bitter. "Of course, by that time there won't be anything left to vote *on,* because those melons are going to get swiped, and LeMan knows it as well as I do. I worked all summer growing them."

"Armel," Maman said sharply, "Icarians don't steal."

Papa spoke. His voice was granite. "I am ashamed of my son. Valmor was a deserter, but I think you're worse. You stay here and undermine the most basic beliefs that we live by. Did you give any thought at all to how your mother and I will

158

face the others after this? I would have been President again next year, but who is going to vote for a man with a deserter *and* a hoarder for sons? I'm thankful at least one of them is an Icarian." He looked at Cabet, who flushed.

"Papa, I don't think you're being very fair to Mel," Cabet said in a near-whisper. "He only wanted to give us a surprise. I'm sure he didn't even think about the principles involved."

Papa's voice rose. "Would *you* have done what he did?"

Cabet glanced at Armel, then lowered his gaze and shook his head slowly.

"Well, thank you one and all for your support!" Armel stood up so abruptly that he knocked the cider mug from Jeannie's hand. "Excuse me, Jeannie, but I've got to get out of here." He slammed into the house, whipped the comforter off the bed in the corner, and slammed back out again. "If anyone wants me," he said with all his dignity, "I'll be sleeping in the library."

He strode across the grass and into the dining hall. At the far end of the room Fremont stood painting, with a ring of lanterns around him to give as much light as possible to the area where he was working. Armel went over and lifted one of the lanterns.

"May I borrow this?" He left before Fremont

159

could answer, and made his way up the circular staircase to the ovenlike heat of the library room. I'll just stay up here till everyone's in bed. Then I'll go down and sleep outside where it's cooler.

He stripped and made himself as comfortable as possible on the hard floor. His mind seethed with anger and helpless frustration, with the pain of Papa's attitude, with the loneliness of belonging now only to himself.

"Come on. Move over. I know you've got one in there." Ignoring her flapping, squawking protests, Armel slipped his hand under the hen. Her feathered underside was warm and sleek against the back of his hand in contrast to the straw and the polished smoothness of the egg. He felt good this morning, braced, ready for the fight.

As he stooped to leave the chicken house, the four youngsters came running across the road toward him, shouting. He raised the egg bucket above his head just in case, and started toward them.

"Mel! Can we have some of your watermelons?"

"Why didn't you tell us you had watermelons? We would have helped you take care of them."

"Papa said they were going to make you go away. They aren't going to make you go away, are they, Mel?"

Rolfe and Emil danced around him as he moved

toward the dining hall, with Gretchen and Louise pressing in close behind.

"Watch out, you kids. I've got eggs in here. I don't know yet what they're going to decide to do with me. They're going to vote next Saturday. And in the meantime, no you may *not* have any watermelons. President LeMan impounded them."

"What does that mean?"

"It means nobody gets any until they decide whether I'm the rightful owner or not. Even *I* don't get any."

Gretchen's round moon face appeared under his elbow. "Maman said you did the worst thing anybody in Icaria could do." Her voice was haughty with disapproval copied from her parents.

"He did not, either," Louise said hotly.

As they neared the dining hall, Citizen Fremont called to Armel from his cabin door. Armel and the children veered in that direction.

"He did, too," Gretchen yelled. "He hoarded!"

"You don't even know what that means," Rolfe shouted. Gretchen and Louise faced each other with clenched fists and tight angry faces.

Fremont raised his voice but otherwise seemed not to notice the children. "Armel, please tell them at the dining hall that I'll be having my breakfast with Catherine in her cabin. They can bring mine there, when they bring hers."

"He did not," Louise screamed.

Armel looked from the girls to Fremont. "Sure, but why?"

"The painting is finished." Fremont closed the door before Armel could say anything more.

He looked down to find Emil shaking his arm. "Gretchen hit Louise in the stomach and made her throw up. I better hit Gretchen, huh?"

Oh, my God, he thought. The whole world is crazy. He sidestepped the children and ran across the grass toward the cellar door that led to the kitchen. It was a trick he had learned years ago, running so smoothly that not a single egg cracked.

By the end of the day there was a line through Icaria as wide and as unmistakable as a fire ditch. On Armel's side were the handful who said, loudly or secretly, that Armel's four hills of watermelons were not intended as a threat to the Icarian way of life, that he hadn't been very smart but surely hadn't meant any harm, that he had every right to grow the melons and to keep them. This last opinion was held by a very small minority—Armel, the two little boys, and, surprisingly, Citizen Fremont.

Unhappily straddling the line were Maman, Jeannie, Cabet, Berthe, and, Armel sensed, Jules Bettanier, who couldn't quite bring himself to disagree aloud with anything President LeMan said.

All the rest of Icaria lined up behind President LeMan.

Shortly after breakfast, while he was searching through a dim corner of the main barn for something with which to fix the sheep pen gate, Armel turned to find Citizen Bronner gazing at him. Bronner's face was heavy with sorrow. Armel faced him.

Bronner sucked on his pipe, and sucked and sucked until Armel's nerves were raw. "I was very sorry to hear about your trouble, pup," Bronner said slowly.

"But not sorry enough to speak up for me."

"Mel, I'm an old man."

What's that got to do with it? Armel asked silently.

"I'm an old man, and I've spent my life building and defending a way of life that I have always believed, and still believe, is the best possible way for human beings to live together in peace."

He lit his pipe, and this time Armel didn't warn him that he was in the barn.

"Armel, you've always been my favorite here. I asked for you to be assigned to me, when it came time to assign you. Don't laugh at an old man when I say you have been my son." He came closer, and his usually vague eyes held Armel's. "The watermelons may seem like a small thing to you, pup. But if you were right about them, it would mean that

I have spent the only life I have fighting for something that was wrong." Abruptly he turned and made his way around the clutter of the barn, muttering into his pipe, ". . . old man now . . ."

Armel turned toward the wall and clenched his fists hard.

During the days that followed, Armel avoided all of them. He continued to sleep in the library and found work to do as far away from the buildings as possible. He ate his meals wordlessly, aware of the tensions that vibrated through the room when he came in, and ricocheted from the brightly painted walls. Because Fremont now insisted on having all his meals in Catherine Noir's cabin, and because he was one of so few supporters, Armel appointed himself to carry the tray to the cabin at mealtimes. It gave him a feeling of righteousness that helped to offset the misery he felt at the hostile stares of the people who were like mothers and fathers to him.

His own mother said little, but sometimes she touched his shoulder when she passed behind his chair, and every night when he climbed to the library room, he found that someone had been there bringing his hay mattress or clean clothes or apricot bread.

On Wednesday Armel went down to the trestle. Citizen Gentry sat beneath the rim of the riverbank, fishing. Armel slid down beside him and looked past the fishline toward his crop. About half of the ripe melons were gone.

"I'm sorry, Mel," Gentry said quietly. "I try to keep people away, but I can't be here every minute. I suppose some people figure they have a right to take the melons."

Armel sighed and began skipping stones across the narrow river. "That's all right. At least they assigned a guard who would try to be fair. I was afraid they'd give the job to Alexis or somebody like that."

Gentry smiled. He'd always been one of Armel's favorites, one of the younger, brighter men.

"Listen, Mel. I just wanted to say, the more I think about this thing, the more I feel you were right. The seeds were given to you; you did all the work; somehow it just doesn't seem fair to take them all away from you. Would you mind not skipping stones right there? You're scaring off the fish."

"Sorry."

"That's all right. Oh hell." He stood and jammed his pole into the mud. With a quick glance back toward the commune, he said, "Come on. This is ridiculous."

Gentry went over to the vines, picked up a melon, and brought it crashing down on his uplifted knee. He handed a dripping red and green chunk to Armel. "Here, eat hearty. You earned it."

Tension seeped through the commune and boiled to the surface in the dining hall, in the barns and the bedrooms. Jobs were reshuffled when Marie Bettanier refused to work in the sewing room with Citizenne Bronner, and the bakery and the washhouse rang with the shouts of angry women. Food was burned or undercooked, and since this was Citizenne LeMan's week to serve, Armel and his few supporters always got their food after everyone else was served.

Fremont continued to eat in Catherine's cabin. When Armel tried to coax him back to the dining hall, he turned his long face away and stroked his cat's throat.

"After all the work you put in on the murals, don't you even want to give people a chance to compliment you on them? Everyone thinks they're beautiful."

Fremont spun toward him, eyes glittering, the soft planes of his lips clamped hard over words he couldn't say. As Armel backed out of the cabin door, he realized that Fremont's reasons for avoiding the dining hall had nothing to do with the general quarreling.

For the first time in Armel's memory the Saturday night meeting was open to all of Icaria, even the children, right down to the Bettanier baby.

Armel took a seat on the men's side in the front row. Cabet sat directly behind him, with Bronner and Bettanier.

Cabet leaned forward and whispered, "Everybody's here but Fremont."

"I think he's listening outside the window," Armel whispered back. "I heard somebody out there."

"Listen, Mel. I feel awful about all this. I'm sorry I didn't speak up more with Papa."

Armel twisted in his chair to scan the room. From the women's side Maman was looking at him, a sober, supporting look. Jeannie smiled a tight smile and half raised her hand to wave. Only Berthe smiled warmly and definitely at him, but then she smiled constantly at everyone, now that she was pregnant. Near the door, Papa and President LeMan talked quietly.

Finally LeMan moved up through the room and mounted the low platform. He caressed his beard while his eyes skimmed the dining hall.

"Roll call shall be dispensed with tonight. I can see that only one person is absent. The question before us this evening may seem trivial to some. However, let me impress upon you the threat that such an incident can present to our peaceful way of life. There is much more at stake here, Citizens, than a paltry few melons."

Paltry few is right, Armel seethed. If all you prying so-and-sos had left me alone, there'd be a dozen good melons on those vines right now.

". . . consider the principle involved," LeMan was continuing. "If we allow one member to claim even so small a crop as this as his own, there will never be an end to it. Yes, Franz."

Papa stood. Armel held his breath and glued his eyes to that hard, handsome face.

"I want to apologize most sincerely to each of you for the trouble Armel has started. His mother and I have asked ourselves time and again how we failed our children, so that one of them deserts and another hoards. We don't know. We would like to believe this incident was just a bit of thoughtlessness and immaturity on Armel's part. We cannot excuse what he's done. We can only apologize."

Armel's jaw tightened. Oh, no, Papa, he thought furiously. Don't apologize for me. Don't be a martyr and pretend you're taking the blame when you're really not. And there isn't even any blame to take. I didn't do anything really wrong. You're supposed to stand up for me!

President LeMan nodded his acknowledgment to Papa and looked around the room. "Citizen James?"

"I just wanted to say, I don't think Armel Dupree belongs in Icaria. I think he's a danger to us all.

Let's get rid of him."

There was a murmur through the room, but it sounded to Armel more like disapproval of James than of himself.

"There will be no question of 'getting rid' of him," President LeMan snapped. "We can't spare a single member. The only question before us to-night is whether or not Armel has a right to the melons. Gentry?"

Armel turned hopefully toward the tall form in the shadows at the back of the room.

Gentry's voice was strong. "I think this whole thing is ridiculous. The boy didn't take anything away from the rest of us—either work time or land or even seeds. He had every right to those melons. In fact, it's been my opinion for a long time, but I just didn't have the courage to say so, that we'd all be better off if those of us who wanted to work a little harder for some special thing could do so, without having to forfeit what we made or grew to the commune. There's something basically wrong with equalizing us all at the lowest level."

His voice was lost in a rising hum of shock and indignation. Peron and Ponte, inseparable as al-ways, were on their feet protesting. A movement at the window attracted Armel. He turned and saw Fremont's high pale forehead, white in the dusk out-side the window.

"Quiet, please. Quiet, please," LeMan shouted over the din. "Yes, Jules."

Bettanier rose to his feet and waited for the noise to subside. He glanced across the room to Marie, and she smiled and nodded slightly.

He began, in his slow, quiet voice. "I guess it isn't any secret to most of you that all my life I've just wanted one thing. To be President of Icaria. I love this place. It's the only home I've ever known, and the highest thing I can imagine for myself and my family is to be President. But since all this came up, I've been doing some pretty serious thinking about what I believe, deep down. I asked myself what I would have done if someone had given me a pack of watermelon seeds."

He slowed to a stop, looked again toward Marie, then went on. "What I came to, after all that thinking was, I still love Icaria as much as ever, but I think I love it because it's mine, not because it's right. I agree with Citizen Gentry. We've been losing young people just about as fast as they grow up, and I believe that if we don't want Icaria to die, we're going to have to moderate our views and allow some room for the man who wants to do more, and *be* more. That's all I've got to say."

Gratefully Armel thought, Well, there goes his chance of ever being President. Thanks, Jules.

The murmur of protest rose again, but Jules

and Marie smiled at each other across the aisle and ignored it. LeMan called again and again for order, and finally got it.

"There is no point in going off on a tangent. We aren't here to discuss the fundamentals of Icarian law, only to vote on Armel Dupree and his watermelons. Now I believe we'd better go ahead with the voting and quit wasting time with foolish discussions. All those who believe. . ."

Suddenly Armel realized they didn't intend to let him defend himself. He half rose, waving his arm in front of LeMan.

"Armel? Did you have something you wanted to say?"

He was on his feet. "Yes, sir. I'd like to have a chance to explain my side of it, if I may." His voice was polite but firm. A good courtroom voice. He stood taller.

LeMan smiled, humoring a child's whim. "All right, Armel, but keep it brief."

Every face in the shadowy hall was fixed on him. He paused a moment to look at them, unconsciously adding suspense and importance to what he was about to say. His mind went blank for a split second; then the words came.

"I just wanted to say that I never had the slightest intention of undermining the Icarian system. The possibility never occurred to me. And I wasn't trying to be selfish with the melons. I wasn't even going to keep them for myself. They were intended to be a present to my family, because I've never had anything of my own before that I *could* give away.

"The seeds were given to me last spring when I went to Shenandoah. The nurseryman gave them to me. I did all the work of taking care of them all summer, and the only things I ever used that belonged to the commune were the ground under the trestle, which was just going to waste anyway, and a sack of horse manure."

Gretchen and Louise giggled.

"If what I did was a crime, then I'm guilty." With all the dignity he could show, which was an impressive amount, he took his seat. His final words hung in the air. They sounded good, even though they were borrowed from something he'd read once.

The vote was seven in favor of Armel, eight against. It was better than he'd expected.

CHAPTER TWELVE

The rising wind blew a cloud across the moon, blacking out the last bit of light in the library room. Armel lay with his head near the door, feet toward the window, the lower bookshelf crowding him on one side and the stacks and cartons crowding on the other. His hay mattress took up every bit of floor space.

He felt as though he had been lying this way

forever, his head pillowed on a low stack of *Revues,* his feet against the plank wall under the window. It's as black as the inside of a cow in here, he thought. I wish the moon would come back out. Then at least I could watch the tree branches blowing around. It's coming up a storm. Well, that's appropriate.

In the long quiet hours since the meeting broke up, Armel had accomplished more serious thinking than he had believed himself capable of.

He thought about Citizen Bronner standing before a classroom of students in a French university, a young man full of beautiful ideals that ignited at the touch of Étienne Cabet's dream. Bronner standing in the river with his beard tied up, talking to himself; Bronner, the intellectual whose sheep and poultry would long ago have died or strayed if Armel hadn't been there. He remembered Bronner's words. "You young ones are the bright hope of Icaria . . . especially Armel Dupree. . . . You're going to be a leader. . . . The watermelons may seem like a small thing . . . but if you were right about them, it would mean that I've spent the only life I have fighting for something that was wrong."

He thought about Papa, who, as much as Armel hated to admit it, was almost always right and who certainly would not have chosen Icaria and stayed with it all these years if it were not the best way to live.

He thought about Maman grieving when Valmor left, exactly as though he were dead.

He thought about Jeannie, with her secret wish of being able to care for her future husband; and of Cabet, who only wanted to be left alone but no longer had the will to withstand the Icarian vote.

He thought of himself luxuriating in the security of Icaria, beginning not to care how hard he worked at his job, because it didn't matter, really. He remembered the morning Louise had tried to get him to help keep the sows out of her rock garden. The pigs aren't *my* responsibility, Louise. I don't have to do anything to help anyone. It's not my responsibility.

He tried to imagine himself ten years, twenty years from now if he stayed in Icaria. Would he be able to keep his mind free from the insidious softening effect of a life in which no challenges ever needed to be met, and no danger ever threatened? No, he realized with a chilled clarity; it's happened to all of them, Papa, Bronner, Fremont. All good minds, good men. Why should I think I could stay immune? Little by little I'd find myself fitting in, not bothering to question whether it was right or wrong, so long as it was easy. Do I want to be that kind of man?

Finally he tried to imagine his life ten or twenty years from now if he left Icaria and tried to live the way Val was living, but it was beyond the power of his imagination.

The rising wind brought with it the first low rumbles of distant thunder, and the leaves blowing outside the window took on the sound of rain, although the rain hadn't started yet. Armel was brought slowly out of his thoughts by a new sound beneath the rustle of the coming storm. A light hacking sound, a soft moaning, sobbing sound.

He got up and pulled on his pants, cursing himself for not having a lantern or a candle with him. Halfway down the stairs, he stopped and stared.

Even in the dark of the dining hall the figure was unmistakable. He stood at the wall near the door, round shoulders and stomach paunch silhouetted by flickering lightning. His hair stood out from his head like radiating madness. One hand was clenched around a large leather punch. He sobbed as he stabbed again and again at the painted figures on the wall.

Armel lunged down the stairs but then stopped, thought for a minute, and then sat down silently and leaned against the stair rails.

Fremont's arm swung slower and slower until finally he dropped the leather punch and leaned against the gouged boards, spent. Armel went down to him and steered him to a seat on the bottom step. Fremont showed no surprise at seeing Armel. He sat obediently, knees and feet together, hands folded against his legs like a small boy in school. Not knowing what else to do, Armel sat beside him.

"I'm a damned shoemaker, Armel." The words came soft and flat. "For eighteen years I don't have a chance to paint, because somebody needs shoes, the horses need more harness, they vote not to buy me paints because they need seed corn. And then all of a sudden they want murals on their walls"—he faced Armel in a fury of frustration—"and all I can paint is—ugly—stick figures. My hands, they're stiff from the leather work. All the love is gone out of these fingers, Armel. They don't know *how* anymore." The long face was wet with tears.

Leery of Fremont's quicksilver moods, Armel said, "I thought the murals were pretty good."

A long sigh escaped Fremont, deflating him. "You're a peasant. You don't know what art is. A child could have done better." He motioned vaguely around the room, where the history of the world from creation to Icaria was hidden in blackness. "I worked much too fast. These paintings should have taken years. I did them in weeks. I hurried because I was afraid to look back at them and see how bad they were."

While Fremont talked, a part of Armel's mind wondered what had happened to the mutual dislike between them. Maybe because they voted against me tonight, he thinks I'm on the outside, with him and Catherine. Or else he's so worked up he's not even thinking about who I am. Maybe it's just that it's dark in here and he doesn't have to look at me.

Fremont had quit talking and sat staring out through the open door. It was raining now. He seemed in no hurry to leave the dining hall, or to move at all, for that matter.

"Citizen Fremont, why did you come with the Icarians in the first place?"

"I came along because I wanted time to paint. Back in France I always had to think about making a living. Then Étienne Cabet came along and said, 'Fremont, pack up your brushes and come to America with us. We are going to found a paradise on earth. There will be rich fields, prosperous factories, good sturdy homes filled with beautiful things. We'll have a university, parks, amusement places, art galleries. Every Sunday we'll have music, theatricals, ballet. We need artists, musicians, scholars. You'll have time to paint and ample opportunities to exhibit.' "

They were silent for a long time, while Armel's mind circled back to his own problem, his own personal weighing of the Icarian dream and his future.

"I can understand why someone like you would come. And Citizen Bronner, because he's such a dreamer. And of course it's easy to see why the good-for-nothing ones like Alexis and Peron and

Ponte stay on here. They'd starve anyplace else, they're so bone lazy. But"—he paused to think out his words—"it's the men like Papa that I still can't figure out, Fremont. He and I don't get along, but still Papa is intelligent and hardworking and practical, and he was a success back in France when he was a lawyer. Why would he deliberately—"

Fremont snorted. "A success, yes. Your papa was a great successful lawyer. Very clever."

Armel strained to see Fremont's face in the dark. "There was some trouble that Papa was in, wasn't there? Do you know what it was?"

"I know what it was."

"Tell me, Jean." Silence. "Citizen Fremont, it's important to me. Please. I have to make up my mind one way or the other, pretty soon now, whether to get out of Icaria or stay here and try to help hold it together. But I need to know whether Icaria is right, whether Papa joined because it is right or because he was running away from something."

"Your papa defended a man."

"Was his name Shagnon?"

"Something like that, I believe. He was charged with kidnapping a little girl. Your papa defended him so brilliantly that he was freed, and a month later Shagnon kidnapped another little girl. She was found dead. It was an ugly thing, with details I couldn't tell you. Some people blamed your papa, but he had only done his job, and they couldn't do anything to him. But after that he lost heart, and when the Icarian movement began, he joined. I didn't know him very well."

Fremont talked on, but Armel didn't hear him. So that was the Shagnon case. Papa defended a guilty man so well that the man was freed to kill a little girl. Poor Papa, who never admits to even a small mistake.

While the rain whispered outside and Fremont talked on, Armel began to understand his father. Papa didn't join the Icarians because he believed the philosophy, or because he thought this was the only right way to live. And I don't think it was because of public feeling against him. Papa may be a lot of things, but I don't think he's that kind of a coward. I'll bet he was afraid of something else—of the responsibility. The responsibility of holding lives in his hands.

A movement at the door interrupted his thoughts. With an irritated maow, the tomcat darted into the room, his coat dark and matted with rain. He gave himself a sketchy tongue-drying, then leaped into Fremont's lap.

"Oh, my poor little tiger, were you lonesome for me? Did you come looking for me?" Fremont's voice dropped to a murmur as he bent himself around the cat.

Armel stood, hesitated for a moment, then climbed the stairs.

When he woke up the next morning, his decision was made. In the wet sunshine it was clear to him that his leaving Icaria was, very simply, a matter of self-preservation. He could see now the truth that had teased and evaded him all summer. If you don't use whatever abilities you have, they rust away and disappear. And if something—like the necessity of making a living—doesn't force you to use them, you probably won't.

He thought about his abilities—a bright, quick mind; the love of winning an argument; a retentive memory that made studying easy. After a few more years of sheep watching, what would that bright mind be like? Bronner's? Fremont's? Even Cabet's? He shuddered. It was too late for them. But not for Armel Dupree.

All he needed now was the right time to tell Maman and Papa. He sat wordlessly with them through breakfast, listening to the conjectures that filled the room. What happened to the wall over there by the door? It's full of choppy places. Whatever could have made holes like that in the wall?

Papa eyed him. "Do you have any idea what happened in here last night, Armel?"

He shook his head.

"You didn't hear anything?"

"I was sleeping pretty soundly."

All morning he hovered around the dining hall, the barns, his parents' house, rehearsing his announcement.

In the afternoon there was a theatrical. They did something Shakespearean; Armel wasn't sure just what it was. He lounged in the doorway of the dining hall, not wanting to commit himself to coming inside and sitting down to watch. Jules Bettanier, Berthe, and Citizen Hawbaker were on the platform gesturing and reading their stilted speeches. The element of farce that they presented was not a part of the play.

As he watched the actors and the audience, Armel felt more strongly than ever that sense of separateness. These people have nothing to do with me. Not really. They think they're living out Étienne Cabet's dream—Icaria, the promised land. Icaria, the cultural center, the good life. But they can't see themselves. They can't see how things really are, or else they'd know it's just a dream.

That night after supper he told them. Walking home from the dining hall with the family, he said, "Could you all come in the front room for a minute? I've got something. . ."

Papa stared hard at him for an instant. Jeannie

kept her face forward but glanced from the corners of her eyes. Berthe and Cabet nodded as they walked. Maman's head jerked; her arms tightened across her stomach as though she'd been punched.

She knows already, he realized. Maybe she knew before I did.

Uneasily they filed into the house. Papa and Maman took the chairs; Jeannie tucked herself down on the bottom step of the stairs; Berthe and Cabet sat on Armel's bed, in the dark corner of the room beside the stairway. Berthe reached for Cabet's hand, but he, unaware of his wife, bent down to scratch his leg.

Armel cleared his throat. He moved to the table at the far side of the little room, and leaned his hip against it. His arms folded themselves casually across his chest, but his fingertips plucked at his shirt, rolling the material in short nervous motions. Papa and Jeannie watched him; Berthe looked at Cabet, and Cab looked at the floor. Maman stared straight ahead, her face turned away from him. Her profile was hard.

"Well, what I wanted to say was—um—I've decided I'd like to go—up to Des Moines for a while and live with Valmor and just sort of see how I like it—up there." He looked directly at Maman. "I found one of Val's letters, Maman, out in the bakery. You should have told me about his offer."

Jeannie was the first to break the electric silence. "Oh, Melly. Leave Icaria?" It was a wail.

He felt he should be saying something more, trying to explain. But how could he ever make any of them understand? What could he possibly say?

Papa came to life then. His voice was like a knife. "Fool! You think you have to go out and conquer the world, don't you? You have to *prove* something. You're not smart enough to appreciate what you have right here under your nose. That out there—that's evil, Armel! Men out there, fighting to get ahead of one another, cutting each other's throats. You want to be a part of that? There's greed out there, boy. Those people are *unhappy* people. They're—"

"Papa. Are the Icarians really any happier, now honestly?" His voice took a shrill edge. "Is Citizen Fremont happy? Is Catherine Noir or Citizen Bronner or you or Maman or the LeMans? Are they really happy, Papa?"

Papa's face reddened. His voice rose. "You young. . . Do you dare to question Icaria? Do you think you're smarter than Étienne Cabet and the rest? Do you presume. . ."

He went on, but Armel's mind grew numb. He stared at Maman's set white profile. She still hadn't looked at him. When Papa's voice finally stopped, Armel said, "I want to be a lawyer, Papa. I don't see that that's so evil. You were one. I feel as though I'd be a good lawyer, a really good one, Papa, and I just can't—not try! I've got to find out for myself if I'm as good as I think I am. I can't just spend the rest of my life taking care of sheep here, and wondering if I could have been a good lawyer. It's what I love doing, Papa."

I know what he'll say, he thought. "How do you know you love doing it when you don't know the first thing—"

"What you love doing! Hah. You don't know the first thing about the practice of law. How do you know what you want and what you don't? You'd hate living in a town, and you'd hate having to work for wages and to worry about how you were going to feed yourself. Stay here, do what you know, let Icaria take care of you. Armel, you can believe me. Icaria is the best way to live. I know. I've lived the other way, and it's no good. Why do you suppose I gave up all I had to join the Icarians? Why?"

There was a hard silence. Armel's eyes locked on his father's. For just an instant Papa's eyes moved nervously under Armel's stare.

He warned himself. No, Armel. Don't say it. Don't hurt him like that. Let him win this one argument. It won't cost you that much.

"Papa, I know you joined Icaria because you believe it's right. And it may be right, but I've got to see for myself how it would be to live someplace else before I can know whether or not this is right for me."

The storm was gathering behind Papa's face. He knows I'm right, thought Armel, and he's furious because he can't think of a good argument.

Papa drew a breath, but before he could speak, Cabet stood up. "Papa, let him go. I just wish I'd had the courage to do that a few years ago."

Small gasps filled the room. All eyes turned toward Cabet as he crossed the room and went into his own parlor, shutting the door quietly behind him. Suddenly Berthe was sobbing. Jeannie ran to her and threw her arms around Berthe's heaving shoulders. Papa slammed out of the house.

Still Maman was unmoved. As Armel went toward her, determined to make her understand that he wasn't really deserting *her,* her lips moved. Almost inaudibly she said, "Two of them. Two of them . . ."

Icaria had rules about severance. Thirty days' written notice must be submitted to the President. At the end of the thirty days, if the deserter still wanted to go, he was given the clothes already in his possession and twenty dollars cash.

It was a month of acute discomfort for Armel. He was given stony looks and curt words by people who had known him since the minute of his birth. Gretchen and Louise hung on him and cried. Catherine Noir appeared at the Dupree door one morning and demanded that Armel give her back her paisley shawl. Citizen Bronner made no effort to hide the hurt he felt at Armel's betrayal. Only the small boys, Rolfe and Emil, seemed to be on his side. They pranced around him, begging him to come back for a visit as soon as possible and tell them what it was like in Des Moines.

He took a last swim in the river, although it was really too cold now. He walked countless fields of the three thousand acres, kicking clods and remembering the time when . . . He went down to the schoolhouse and sat in a back bench while President LeMan lectured the four youngsters. He walked slowly around Catherine's cabin and remembered when it had been home. He patted its rough flank. In a burst of sentimentality he even said good-bye to the graveyard, which he hated.

On October twelfth the thirty days were up. Jules Bettanier had asked for, and received, permission to drive Armel into Corning to the depot. Jules and the light wagon were in front of the Dupree house shortly after breakfast. It was a cool gray morning, with the feel of rain, or possibly even snow, in the air.

Armel stood in front of the house. His luggage

was a pillow slip, one of Maman's two fine embroidered ones she'd brought from France and kept hidden from the Icarians all these years. Inside the pillow slip were his extra clothes, the Iowa law pamphlet, and the twenty dollars.

Jeannie and Berthe hugged him and sniffled in his ear. Cabet shook his hand more firmly than usual and met his brother's eyes. The look wished Armel good luck.

Maman said, "Be careful what you eat. Come back when you can . . ." Her voice choked. She crushed him to her for an instant, then went into the house.

Armel turned to Papa. "Papa?" He offered his hand. It stuck out alone between the two men. Then Papa took it.

"If those law books up in the library were still mine, they'd have made you a nice collection to start off with." He looked directly at Armel, and the flash of understanding that passed between them suddenly eased the weight Armel carried.

He climbed into the wagon, and Jules rippled the reins. As the wagon lurched out onto the road between the dining hall and the barns, the sun burned its way through the overcast. Armel turned to look back. The roofs of the commune, the line of poplar trees in the background, were touched with the sun. The place was a beautiful painting.

Armel's heart contracted. Maybe they're right. Maybe Icaria is the best way.

A train hooted and clacked around the shoulder of the woodlot hill. As Armel turned farther on the wagon seat to catch sight of the train, he saw the familiar bent wisp of Catherine, silhouetted against the gray sky on the crest of the sheep pasture. Her fist was raised in anger at the train. Faintly, over the noise of the train, Armel heard, "Sacré gueulard!"

Poor silly Catherine, trying to shush the trains. He looked at the receding roof of the dining hall. Poor—all of them.

With a pang of disloyalty, and a deep and growing sense of relief, he turned to face the road ahead.

THE END OF THE DREAM

Two years later the commune of Icaria split into two factions—the younger members, or Minority, and the older members, the Majority. The dissension was caused partly by the growing demand of the younger members for private ownership of things such as Armel's watermelons, and partly by the Minority's refusal to accept without question the ruling of their elders.

190

The Majority party members were given land in the east half of Icaria's territory. Here they built another settlement, about two miles southeast of the original commune. Their dining hall has been remodeled and now is used as a farmhouse.

The Minority party remained for a few years at the original commune, then sold out and moved to California, where they formed another society which has since dissolved. Eventually, the remaining Majority members voted to sell the rest of the Iowa land. Some stayed on in the Corning vicinity; others gradually scattered.

So ended the Icarian dream.

ABOUT THE AUTHOR

Lynn Hall's interests are young people, dogs, and horses—in that order. She makes her living writing books for young readers, and her three main interests figure prominently in her stories. Her earlier books are: *The Shy Ones, The Secret of Stonehouse,* and *Ride a Wild Dream.*

Miss Hall has lived in Denver, Ft. Worth, Louisville, Chicago, and Des Moines, and she has worked as a telephone operator, a veterinarian's assistant, a handler of show dogs, and an advertising copywriter. None of her varied activities, however, brought her complete satisfaction until she began to write books a few years ago.

Miss Hall lives near the village of Garnavillo, in northeast Iowa. Between books, she reads or sketches or explores the nearby hills and woodlands with a dog or two at her heels.